I0720843

THE RAZ/SHUMAKER PRAIRIE SCHOONER
BOOK PRIZE IN FICTION

Editor

Kwame Dawes

Invitation

STORIES

Mi Jin Kim

UNIVERSITY OF NEBRASKA PRESS

Lincoln

The University of Nebraska Press is part of a land-grant institution with campuses and programs on the past, present, and future homelands of the Pawnee, Ponca, Otoe-Missouria, Omaha, Dakota, Lakota, Kaw, Cheyenne, and Arapaho Peoples, as well as those of the relocated Ho-Chunk, Sac and Fox, and Iowa Peoples.

For customers in the EU with safety/GPSR concerns, contact:
gpsr@mare-nostrum.co.uk
Mare Nostrum Group BV
Mauritskade 21D
1091 GC Amsterdam
The Netherlands

LIBRARY OF CONGRESS CATALOGING-IN-PUBLICATION DATA
Names: Kim, Mi Jin, 1986- author
Title: Invitation: stories / Mi Jin Kim.
Description: Lincoln: University of Nebraska Press, 2025 | Series: The Raz/Shumaker Prairie Schooner book prize in fiction
Identifiers: LCCN 2024056857
ISBN 9781496244345 paperback
ISBN 9781496244628 epub
ISBN 9781496244635 pdf
Subjects: BISAC: FICTION / Short Stories (single author) | FICTION / Literary | LCGFT: Short stories
Classification: LCC PS3611.I454538 I58 2025 | DDC 813/.6—dc23/eng/20250328
LC record available at https://lccn.loc.gov/2024056857

Designed and set in Arno Pro by Katrina Noble.

for my mother, for Liz

Just as life had been strange a few minutes before, so death was now as strange. The moth having righted himself now lay most decently and uncomplainingly composed. O yes, he seemed to say, death is stronger than I am.

—Virginia Woolf, "The Death of the Moth"

CONTENTS

ACKNOWLEDGMENTS

I am indebted to so many teachers and mentors, my friends and family. Special thanks go to Jeff Henebury for his brilliant insights and to the Helen Zell Writers' Program.

Thank you to judges Laird Hunt and Elizabeth Crane for this honor. And of course, my heartfelt gratitude toward Kwame Dawes, Siwar Masannat, Courtney Ochsner, Anne McPeak, Abbey Frankforter, and Taylor Martin at Prairie Schooner / the University of Nebraska Press.

Invitation

Acapulco

I knew when Hojun's mother disappeared, more or less, because she, or someone with her phone, texted back to my question of tacking on an extra 150,000 won to her son's monthly tuition fee for an international shipment of books we needed and then—nothing. The family was upper–middle class so I felt comfortable billing them like this occasionally, but also I was resentful of them precisely because they were upper–middle class and pretended to me that either they didn't know, or couldn't do, something like ordering their own books for the one son they were supposed to be rearing. In this country, such people could pay anyone to do anything for them.

I had seen and interacted in person only with the mother and son but I had a good sense of what sort of father was involved—an older man, probably, someone who didn't work very much but whose work brought in all the money; his hands-off, distant and indifferent, even willfully ignorant and uninterested paternal style was likely supported by his circle and, of course, this sort of thing was still culturally encouraged. Hojun, as the product of this type of father and the kind of mother I knew the woman to be, had turned out exactly as you'd expect from this grotesque and far too common familial arrangement. He was a humorless and subtly defiant child; to me he was mostly cold and frequently cranky. I found him to be intellectually mediocre, the type of student I would have preferred not to take on if it had been up to me. My friends claim not to understand me when I say this sort of thing, that I truly can't help but take on any prospective who comes along, but it's true: I don't always need the money, and I'd be much better off not working with anyone else's child. Long after I discovered the truth of what had likely happened to his mother, I became more certain about my stance on odd and unpleasant children and what I should do about them. But at the time, I disliked Hojun from the onset and still agreed to teach him what I could.

The day after his mother supposedly disappeared, he showed up for our tutoring session at seven o'clock. I disliked him even more because he encroached on my evenings in this way while all my other students had nicely open weekends. Only this one had such a packed schedule we had to meet on his Tuesday and Thursday evenings, seven o'clock, and at my apartment because he lived close enough that he could walk over from his luxury town house. I couldn't eat dinner before he arrived, because then I'd have to floss and brush my teeth before our sessions—but what if I wanted to snack on something later? I'd have to drink tea while he was here, which would stain my teeth if I brushed right before I had my evening cup. After he left it would be too late in the day to sit down to a full meal; ravenous as I was after working with a student, I couldn't break my diet and hope to keep slim while maintaining such a sedentary life at my desk, in my little apartment, only taking walks when I felt up to sketching in my eyebrows and putting on actual shoes instead of the plastic slippers I wore to take the food waste out to the bins.

I dreaded seven o'clock; twice a week I waited for it to come, pacing on my balcony. That day when he arrived, neither of us knew yet that his mother had left the family. At the end of our lesson, Hojun informed me that she hadn't been home when he got back from his after-school academy. I didn't care about the comings and goings of his mother and was annoyed that he thought I would be interested. "I'm sure she's just busy," I said, walking him to the door. Hojun was a little fat, which I found suspicious. Usually boys of his class and type were naturally thin, or burned off the expensive fruit and imported milk and high-quality beef their mothers fed them by running around everywhere as soon as they were dismissed from their lessons. A clever child could always surprise me, offer something new that only someone so young and little could notice or think about. But almost right from the beginning, Hojun made our lessons unendurable. He moved slowly and spoke slowly but only when I asked him a question. He almost never answered immediately but only after asking for clarification, because he hadn't been listening or hadn't understood though I always spoke plainly to him. I hated waiting for him to speak, but I also hated listening to him when he did.

"See you Thursday," I said, hurrying him out of my apartment with my eyes. We'd only just ended our lesson but already I dreaded seeing him again.

Thursday evening, at seven o'clock, Hojun showed up at my door, perfectly on time. He looked a little odd, though it was hard to tell, exactly, with little boys, the intensity and quality of their grievances. I dismissed whatever I was seeing. I thought I might be imagining it.

About fifteen minutes into our session, however, he explained the situation to me with his chair turned toward the wall, carefully giving me sidelong glances while he spoke though usually I had to practically shout at him to get direct eye contact for longer than ten seconds. Like all small, stupid, and dangerously overindulged children he took forty seconds to explain that his mother hadn't come home, though it should have taken him about four. While he was (slowly) speaking I put on a look of teacherly concern in case he told his father about me. I was always thinking of how I might be accused or slandered while I taught children, which made the job much more taxing than it should have been. It was work that made you paranoid and deceitful because all children are liars. If a child was stupid, too, like Hojun, you had to be on guard for the worst. If for whatever reason you must interact with children in some capacity, as I do, you have to mind your face and your expressiveness, check your natural responses, be sober and suspicious about everything, even in regard to what a child might refer to as a joke. People who don't teach don't know this and refuse to believe me, but smiling overlong or frequently is intolerable to all children; frowning, furrowing the brow, narrowing the eyes—these are the only acceptable expressions of feeling. Also, you have to leave paper trails. It doesn't matter how young or old the child is, for all brats are capable of subterfuge, and their motives for lying don't have to be rock solid when it comes to accusing someone being paid to educate them. Nowadays when it comes to a student and teacher, the burden of proof is almost never on the younger though of course it should always be the other way around, regardless of the consequences of disbelieving children, as a rule; in my experience, most students, maybe all, are aware of the incredibly stupid ideas people have about children in our world. You won't last long in the teaching profession unless you're ready to arm yourself against cruelty and criminality each time you sit before a child and give them your attention.

During our lesson I dealt with Hojun as if I felt something about his situation, though I could hardly stand him by the time our two hours came to an end.

"I'm sure your mother is fine," I said when our time was up, adding a few clichés about parents and their eternal devotion to their children. I hoped Hojun wasn't comforted by my words. I hoped I worried him more with the deliberately false tone I adopted.

When I'd been a bit younger than Hojun, my mother had abandoned my father and me and gone to live with her sister for a year. I knew the disturbance and pain of Hojun's mother leaving him like this, even if it turned out to be temporary, would never heal. It was a thing unlike any other in existence, a mother willingly going away from you.

"I'll speak to your father tomorrow for you," I said carelessly. "Maybe he'll tell me more than he's willing to share with you."

This was a grand gesture I was making, and totally unnecessary, unhelpful even. The next day I forgot all about what I'd told Hojun; I had lots to do, errands I'd been putting off because of the heat wave. I woke up early, treated myself to a pancake breakfast at McDonald's, then went grocery shopping at the big box store in the next town over. As I was stepping out of the bus I noticed a new coffee place and, because the day was already so warm and muggy, got myself an overpriced iced caramel macchiato. It was a shop that sold both coffee and knitwear, specifically handmade cup sleeves; while I looked through their ugly things I entertained the idea of billing Hojun's parents for food and drink, consumed by myself or by Hojun (he disliked the water from my LG purifier [he said they drank only out of plastic bottles at home, which, whether true or false, struck me as one of the most troubling family customs I'd ever heard of] and preferred fruit juice or soda). I had never been paid extra by Hojun's parents for all the little things he used while in my apartment—my beverages, my toilet paper and napkins, pencil lead, scratch paper. I wondered at myself. I could endure unpleasantness for money, but I was practically paying the family back whenever I played hostess while he was over. That sort of thing needed to end, and fast, I decided. I owed nothing to this boy—and I wasn't even expected to teach him anything special, really. We all knew it, including Hojun. His family paid me because it was all just part of how things were done. It wasn't so different from how we sometimes tossed our trash right on the street, telling ourselves other people were paid by the city to pick it up. But it *wasn't* part of how things were done to give an ungrateful boy food and drink out of my own refrigerator, my sink, and my cabinets; and the next time he needed to use the toilet, I decided, I'd tell him to go downstairs and use the open restroom on the first floor, the one the building's custodial staff used. Even the water he used out of my pipes was suddenly, to my mind, very precious to me.

Not long after Hojun told me about his mother's disappearance, I learned why she'd seemingly abandoned her son and husband.

I was informed of the situation by a former colleague who also taught the boy and was better connected to the family. It turned out the couple had been at each other's throats for a while. They'd battled it out over the course of the year; finally, the father had elected to stay and care for the boy, while they agreed that the mother could do as she wished, and where she wished. Usually this wasn't a surprise or even much of an issue for the child long-term if the man's mother or sister or some other relative were in the picture, but that was not the case here, my colleague told me. There was no one in Hojun's father's life, no other maternal figure to speak of. It was the woman who had all the money and accomplishments, and she came from a well-connected family. She was going to be fine, the colleague told me; he'd heard she'd gone abroad somewhere on holiday. Who knew when or if she'd be back?

Hojun showed up for our Tuesday evening session although I'd fully expected our sessions to stop while his family was dealing with their crisis. With his mother out of the country, I had little faith in a father keeping up with his son's tutors and academies. I assumed he wouldn't know the first thing about my fees, or about me at all. But on Monday morning someone deposited my fee into my account; and there the boy was at my door on Tuesday evening, at seven o'clock. To my surprise, Hojun looked pretty normal; his father had done a good job supervising his washing and dress. He had done all his reading homework; he was not fussy or moody. He silently worked on his essay on North American coastlines while I read a novel. At one point he looked up at me from his writing, the eraser tip of his Japanese lead pencil between his lips.

"Yes?" I said.

He shook his head. "Never mind."

When it came to a student, I treated interruptions and pauses in the flow of work severely. I said we couldn't continue unless he came out with it.

"What's so important, Hojun?"

He said it was nothing, which I rewarded by letting him continue without a lecture about distractions and discourtesy. During our break, upon returning from the bathroom—though I'd wanted to, I couldn't bring myself to order him down to the janitors' restroom— Hojun accepted my glass of apple juice without thanks, which he'd never done before. I kept an eye on his face as I had him read aloud from the next unit in our book. When I finally caught a little quiver in his lip, I stopped him mid-sentence.

"What's the problem?"

The boy blew out his breath but wouldn't speak.

"Is this about your mother?"

He nodded.

"And?"

"I don't know."

"Tell you what: we can talk about this, or we can stop wasting my time and I'll send you home." This wasn't much of a threat, but I suspected Hojun didn't want to be reminded of his mother's absence and preferred even my busywork over going home.

"My mom won't text me back," Hojun said finally.

I gently tapped him on the head with a piece of paper. "She's abroad, silly. Maybe she doesn't have Wi-Fi, or she turned off her phone."

"Actually," Hojun said, "my mother is dead." He wiped his nose with the back of his hand. "I know because I saw it happen."

"Nonsense," I said, and quickly prompted him to read the next paragraph. He wouldn't. He looked at me without expression.

"I wished it into a bowl of water and then I drank the water."

"What did you wish into a bowl of water, Hojun?"

"To talk to my mom."

It sounded to me like one of those internet "magic spells" so popular with elementary and middle school kids. With boys they usually tried it out in pairs or groups, and it almost always had to do with "conjuring" ghosts or entering some parallel dimension. It struck me as very in-character for Hojun to try something out like this alone, and for such a preposterous purpose.

Hojun said nothing and focused on the page again. But he didn't read. Nor did I prod him to. I looked at him in cold silence until he looked up at me. His eyes were wet.

I tapped our book with my ballpoint pen. "You're wasting my time, Hojun. And yours, if you care about that sort of thing."

He wouldn't return to his work. He began crying silently, hiding his face behind his book. I took my time getting out a package of wet wipes from my bathroom cabinet. I allowed him three sheets, which he took respectfully with both hands. I sat in the chair beside his, rather than my usual one across the table, and watched him cry. He wiped his raw eyes but didn't blow his nose.

"Class is over," I said. I glared at him as he looked at the clock, which clearly read five till. Sometimes children argued when I did this, the prissy little pedants. But Hojun only silently gathered up his things and walked to the door. "Look," I said, "has your father explained things? I mean, *properly*, about what's going on between him and your mother?" I asked.

The boy shook his head, though I wasn't sure he understood what I was really saying.

"Well, I'm sure your mother will come back and see you any day now. I know she misses you very much."

Again he shook his head.

"What do you mean by that, Hojun? No, you don't think she misses you?"

Rather than answering a question he disliked or didn't understand, the boy waited, like all children spoiled by the empty-headed mothers of this generation, for me to stop requiring his participation. That was how Hojun concluded our conversations: by waiting me out.

I didn't care whether he spoke or not; I was tired of him now and wanted him out of my apartment.

I wanted to yawn but knew better than to show him so much of the inside of my mouth. "You know, as we speak, your mother might be on a fabulous vacation—Acapulco, even, just like we're learning about." It was the wrong season for the area, but in my view, anywhere was better than this damp and distressed part of the world. I hated summers here; though I kept the air conditioning on twenty hours out of the day, everything in the apartment eventually grew mildewy. "Isn't it beautiful out there in the world, Hojun? Wouldn't you want your mother to be somewhere like that, enjoying herself?"

He didn't even shrug a response; he only looked up at me, waiting to be dismissed.

"If you keep acting so strangely with me, Hojun, I'll have to tell your father," I said. "Off you go then."

The boy didn't come to class that Thursday evening. On Friday, around noon, I received a text from an unknown number. The sender introduced himself to me as Hojun's father. He subtly referenced his family's present difficulties, which was why he was discontinuing his son's sessions with me, he wrote, but I could keep my fee for the rest of the month. There was more to the message, but the implication that I would want to keep the money despite having just been released from my obligations irked me. I replied immediately, asking for his bank account number. A minute later, he called me up. Hojun's father spoke much too carefully and brightly; I found myself echoing his cheerful tone though normally I spoke to parents harshly and coldly—mothers liked that sort of thing, because they needed their children to not like me very much. I was unused to speaking to fathers and wasn't sure, even after assessing him for a minute or two, what I needed to do to claim authority in our conversation.

"I'm sorry if I'm putting you out," he said, "but I'm afraid I won't take the money back. You requested reimbursement from my wife, didn't you? We owe you some money for Hojun's books?"

"It's not a problem," I said.

"If you could be so kind as to . . . in fact, you'd be helping us out if you accepted the money. My wife would've sent you something for the upcoming holiday, as thanks for all your hard work this year. Do you see?"

I thought about mentioning his son's bizarre fantasy about his mother being dead. A week was much too short a time for a child to start lying about his mother's existence. But all at once I realized it didn't matter, really, what was wrong with the boy or the mother or both: I was free of Hojun now. My Tuesdays and Thursdays were mine again. Hojun's family had given me a gift, really. So after some hemming and hawing, more for the sake of my own image than out of any consideration for his father, I ended the call.

Some weeks later I saw Hojun in the neighborhood. We were a couple of blocks from my apartment, and only a block from his. The better stores were on their end of the neighborhood, small but nicely stocked boutiques and specialty shops I stopped in sometimes on my way home from the subway station. That evening I was picking up a custom fruit basket for an acquaintance who'd connected me to several students that year. I was in a good mood when I ran into the boy; I greeted him with uncalled-for enthusiasm. "Hojun!" I said, waving madly at him as if he were an idiot dog for whom only big, clownish gestures and oafish shouting were intelligible. His father came out of a store just as the boy was tipping his head at me and I, feeling self-conscious standing before a parent, clumsily and foolishly said a few nice things to the boy and asked about his school subjects. Before we were even introduced, I sensed the father was wary of me and would want to cut the conversation short. I had never seen the father in person since I'd only ever dealt with the mother. We had, of course, spoken just that once, on the phone; but the man who came upon me that evening, taking me in so suspiciously, so guardedly, was more or less exactly the sort of person I'd envisioned from the false tones of his voice. When I confirmed for him who I was and what I did for his son, he smiled nervously and pretended to be pleased to make my acquaintance; as I asked after him and the boy, he looked past me and around us, as though he were looking for someone. "I'm double parked," he said, pointing at the white BMW idling just behind me. "We'll have to be going now." I tipped my head at them and, feeling insulted, watched them go, noting how Hojun didn't bother acknowledging me again before getting into his father's car.

I recalled the offense when Hojun showed up at my apartment the next day. He didn't have his backpack, which, for just a moment, gave him the look of a being entirely new to me, some strange carefree child I hadn't had to deal with before. I popped my gum at him as he explained—unasked—how he spent his Sunday afternoons alone now, for his father usually went out at this time and he had no tutoring scheduled for himself. I panicked upon hearing this even as I invited him in. I thought perhaps his father had changed his mind and had sent him over to resume our lessons.

Without asking, Hojun sat at my dining table in his usual seat. I poured him a glass of grape juice, then waited for him to explain himself further.

He didn't; he drank and drank and then asked for a second glass. I poured it for him. "Hot out, isn't it?" I said. "You should've stayed indoors. They issued a warning about the temperature this morning. *All children and old folks . . .*" I knew I'd have to walk him home, or risk Hojun fainting somewhere on my apartment grounds. But I loathed the idea of entertaining him for even a quarter of an hour, unpaid. I decided to speed things up.

"You can't stay long, Hojun. I have an appointment with another student coming up."

He looked into his drained glass. "Oh," he said, after some contemplation.

He wasn't getting the hint. I tapped the table thrice with my fingers, to call his attention. "It was good to see you last night."

"Oh, yeah."

"And it was nice to meet your dad finally."

Hojun shut his eyes but kept his face turned openly toward me. It was one of the few perks of teaching someone else's children, these studies I could make of a small human face at its most honest and unselfconscious; after a moment I grew tired of it, however, and got up to wash my hands at the kitchen sink.

"How are you guys doing?" I asked. "You and Dad?"

He shrugged.

"Has your mother called?" When he didn't answer, I turned off the faucet and gave him a stern look. "Are you mad at her, Hojun?"

The boy frowned. "What do you mean?"

"I mean, are you upset with your mom for leaving you?"

"I told you," he said, after a moment, blinking. "My mother is dead."

I crossed my arms over my chest. "Hojun, I told you I don't like this kind of talk." I dried my hands on too many paper towels, which annoyed me. I laid them out to dry on my counter, to reuse later. "Why have you come to see *me*?"

He shrugged, staring down at his hands. A softer woman, a good teacher, would have reached out to reassure him. Instead of comforting him, however, I collected his empty glass and scrubbed it with hot water and a spritz of vinegar. I wanted not a trace of him left on my glassware.

"Come—I'll have to walk you home now. It's what your father would want."

He followed me out of the apartment without protest. Neither of us spoke until we reached the crosswalk.

"Hojun, who told you to wish your questions into a bowl—"

"I saw it on YouTube."

"But what do the bowl and water have to do with anything?"

After a moment he said, "You make your wish, then you drink the water. The water's supposed to get digested. Then you go to sleep and you dream about what you wished for."

"So it was a dream?"

"My father killed my mother," Hojun said without emotion. He was watching the cars pass. Then the cars all came to a stop. The sign flashed green before us.

"How did he do it?"

"They were in a car. But it didn't look like our car. It was smaller, with white seats, not black, like my dad's. They were talking. My mom was crying. But she was mad, too. All of a sudden he hit her on the head, over and over again. He looked for something bigger or something, I couldn't see what it was. He poked a hole into her face with it. Then he poked holes all over her arms, because she was holding them up, like this, in front of her." A motorcyclist disregarded the light and sped past us. I put a hand out to stop Hojun but he continued walking without looking. I guided the boy safely across the road and pulled him to a bench where I sat him down.

I looked into his flushed face, forcing eye contact though he dropped his gaze after only a second.

"The scarier or more shocking something is, the better we remember it. You'll realize when you're older how meaningless all this stuff is, how silly it is to spend time worrying about what you saw while you were asleep, Hojun, so put it out of your mind."

He was breathing heavily; I looked around us, wary of causing a scene in the middle of a bustling neighborhood. But no one was paying us any attention.

I thought of something: "Who else have you talked to about this?"

He shook his head.

"Is that no, you don't want to tell me? Or no, you haven't told anyone?"

He nodded, once.

I patted his shoulder roughly. I wished not to touch him but it was the only thing I could think to do. He felt like something being steamed in a muslin sleeve. I walked him off the bench and down the street until I couldn't take the heat and humidity anymore. We stopped in at an unmanned ice cream shop; I looked around for the cheapest items and bought him something melon-flavored. "For you," I said. "Forget all about it now."

Hojun held on to his popsicle without opening it. It was melting into soup inside its plastic by the time I dropped him off at the gate to his complex. He still had it in his hand, unopened, as I guided him away from me. "Until next time," I called out.

Some weeks later I caught a lucky break and was connected to a job at a private school in another province. I took the opportunity to pack up my life and move out of the neighborhood as fast as I could. On the day before I was to leave, I thought of Hojun. I'd found our books, including the ones on Mexico, and wondered if his mother had finally come home. I called his father.

"That's right, I never updated you about her," he said. "Knowing how much our family likes you, I'm sure we've told you too much about things you couldn't possibly be interested in."

I said it was fine; I would have gone on to say he didn't need to reassure me in this way, but he was speaking very quickly and I couldn't get a word in.

Also: he seemed to find something a little funny, or perhaps I was confused about what I thought I was hearing.

"My wife is good," Hojun's father said. "She returned to school—graduate studies. Returned to that part of her life. She'd studied abroad when she was younger. Stopped all that when she married me. We'd been trying for a child for years before Hojun finally came. Did you know?"

I admitted I knew nothing about her. "But thank you. How good of you to tell me." I chewed the inside of my cheek. I felt I ought to say something kind or authoritative; instead I asked how Hojun was taking everything.

"Taking what?"

"The separation," I said. I'd almost stammered but caught myself. The one thing I did well was talk as though nothing and no one could ever bother me; it'd gotten me far, despite everything about my person and my persona working against me. It troubled me whenever someone was able to fluster me as Hojun's father did, so I quickly changed the subject.

I gave him one of the old standbys I used whenever I wanted to cut a conversation short with a parent: I told him I expected his son to grow up to be a brilliant student. "He's funnier than you'd think, and very imaginative," I said, which was something I said about all of them. "Very creative. I think he might do well to study humanities. Go into law, maybe, or marketing. Though finance wouldn't be too surprising."

The father, as I expected, was not interested in hearing this. He apologized and said he had to go; I parroted his words and said I, too, had an appointment.

"I wish you both well," I said warmly. "Hojun was one of my absolute favorite students." Unsurprisingly, his father didn't even thank me for the compliments. He expected them, of course, but also didn't want to acknowledge that it took effort for me to pay them. After exchanging brusque farewells, we hung up. Then I blocked his number—as well as his mother's and Hojun's—from my phone.

The next morning, before driving away with the movers, I tossed my students' books into the communal recycling bin. I held on to the last one; it was Hojun's, its cover featuring a heavily Photoshopped beach vista in Acapulco. I wondered where it was his mother had gone to study, if it could be true that she'd chosen her midlife crisis of self-fulfillment, or whatever it was she thought she wanted, over her son. I knew some mothers could be happier without their children.

My questions about her state of mind reminded me of other stories and scenarios, distressful things I wished not to think about. Hojun, too, I hoped not to remember. One day soon he would, I predicted, tell a more appropriate person about the things he'd told me. Then, unlike most lost little children, he'd get the help he needed.

Family Portrait

That morning Gitae's wife went out early with her girlfriends. In his mind this meant he'd gotten "stuck" with the kids, but he also knew he was repeating conventions he didn't actually believe. Like all reasonable family men and women his age, he knew the kids were half his, half his responsibility. But for Gitae, this was easier to intellectualize than it was to believe. What it felt like *emotionally* to him that Saturday morning was that his wife really was "sticking it" to him for working so much during the week, and for having his Sundays mostly to himself because of his wife's and children's church schedules. When he was at home he was required only to physically be present with the children. Six—but usually it was all seven—days out of the week, his wife also worked as a freelancer at home so she could keep an eye on the children, but she took care of the household along with her work responsibilities, and anything that might come up or need to be addressed: family celebrations and school or academy events; their children's education and doctor's visits. Gitae knew he could try harder. So they'd agreed that Saturday mornings were "hers," while Sundays were his. But for some reason he still thought this arrangement unfair.

Her text messages woke him: his wife had sent him photos of her brunch and the three girlfriends she'd gone out with. Industrious bitch, he thought sleepily to himself.

He knew he was nothing like his father, a man so stunted physically and emotionally that after about the sixth grade Gitae stopped having anything in common with him, and, growing up, he could no longer be reprimanded without both father and son walking away with injuries. They'd stopped speaking to each other almost entirely the year before he went off to finish his military service; two years later his father was dead.

Nowadays, the sort of father he'd had was a near-mythical figure among his own friends and acquaintances; however, whenever the subject of fatherhood came up with his wife or with his friends, Gitae felt that he ought not to say anything about how his old man had been with him. He was not ashamed of or ambivalent about his childhood, but he disliked the idea of other people making up their own opinions about how it might have been, and why he was the way he was now.

But he thought about his father often. He'd been remembering something from his earlier years that Saturday morning, just before he'd collapsed. After he'd gotten the kids their breakfast, he asked for exactly fifteen minutes of their best behavior, which he promised to reward with an afternoon frolic at the city's kite festival. Gitae had just gotten out of the shower and was searching for the blow dryer when he was struck by what he later explained to himself as an inexplicable bout of vertigo. As he gripped the edge of the dresser, reorienting his sense of up and down and willing himself not to vomit, the children came into the room, bored, restless, and whining about how long he was taking to get ready. He continued to search the drawers as they looked on; for some reason it was the height of comedy to them whenever the towel was about to slip from his waist. The boy laughed with such zeal the phlegmy scum in his throat, which they hadn't been able to treat despite four trips to the ENT, was finally cracked and loosened. After the boy was done wiping his snot on his mother's pillow, he began tumbling on the bed while his sister, a follower rather than a leader though she was two years older, jumped up after him and began leaping from corner to corner. "Not on the pillows, guys, please," their father said, holding his towel up around his hips. The last thing he remembered doing before dropping to the floor was looking at his reflection in the mirror and finding it odd, the wetness of his hair, and the moisture in his eyes. *You can't do any better*, he thought to himself, then fell, as they told him later, right where he stood, unconscious.

Gitae's stay in the hospital was brief and far less relaxing than if he'd simply stayed at home to recuperate. After he was admitted they gave him a series of tests for which he had to report for in various rooms around and across the building, going up two floors for a CT scan, then down to the first for blood and urine samples. Until they unhooked him from his IV he had to wheel it around to get from elevator to room and out of it again; though there were plenty of other patients on any given floor doing the same thing, he felt underdressed in his hospital grays, and was self-conscious about clutching his pole. Apart from the chill he took at the hospital, sleeping a sort of half-sleep in a small room he shared with a middle-aged patient who shockingly went about barefooted, Gitae felt *fine*, and the tests backed him up on this eventually, telling him nothing he didn't already know about himself—he was pre-diabetic, generally unfit, should stop drinking, et cetera. They asked him a lot of questions about his morning and the evening before, because it sounded as though he'd had a mild seizure, or a reaction to something he'd eaten or drunk. He could have woken up with low blood pressure and his hot shower might have exacerbated things. Everything they told him was inconclusive, theoretical, and possible, they told him, because people collapsed for all sorts of reasons. He was discharged the next morning.

As soon as Gitae was in his own clothes and following his wife and kids to their car in the visitors' lot of the hospital grounds, he felt mostly normal again. The incidents of the day before were like someone else's story or a scenario he had pictured in his mind. He didn't want to remember it; what was most clear to him was that even a single night's stay in a hospital room was something he wished never to have to experience again until he was much, much older or else too weak or injured or sick to know or want better.

He took his family for a "recovery brunch" to the rooftop garden restaurant of the H—Hotel, one of the children's favorite places in the city. Over peony waffles and honeybee tea his little girl, at his prompting, explained once again how, when Gitae had collapsed, she'd very calmly called the police while the boy had helped her hold the phone.

"Brava," the children's mother said. "And for you, sir, magnifico," she added, for the boy's sake.

"When it happened," Gitae said, "did you guys worry I might *die*?" His wife shot him a dark look.

But their little boy only shrugged, which his sister copied. The kids got up and, shrugging exaggeratedly at each other, giggled and ran off to look at the various new summer things growing and blooming in the greenhouse.

After brunch, his wife waited in line behind a dozen other similarly-styled mothers (wispy bangs and low chignons were in that summer) and their one or two beautifully dressed children for their turn to take family photos under the arched trellis. Gitae walked off to use the toilet; his in-laws phoned as he was returning. He took the call standing beside a fake pear tree, fingering a family of plastic ladybugs "climbing" up the bark. They weren't able to come up that morning to see him, his wife's mother said, but promised to reward the children for keeping calm during his "illness" with a trip to the new dinosaur-themed amusement park later that summer. How *were* the children doing? his mother-in-law asked a second time.

"Oh, they're fine, I think," Gitae said. "If it'd been their *mom* . . ."

"All children love their mothers more," she said quickly, then began talking of some people she knew and their precocious grandchildren, slyly hinting, as usual he supposed, that he and his wife should add a few more academies to their children's schedules, make them learn German or Japanese before they'd even finished their first English camps.

"No one seems to know what's wrong with me," he said when he could get a word in. This set off a fresh chain of questions (rhetorical) and comments, observations and dietary recommendations. His mother-in-law promised to send him some herbal supplements, though she added, as they were hanging up, how you couldn't be sure where they were sourcing the antlers these days.

"Could be just ground-up twigs and weeds," she said. "Everything's shipped in from overseas, but as long as they bottle it up in the country they can slap on the domestic label. I don't even know if you'll take well to antler—have you had it before? My daughter says you refuse the supplements and health food she orders for you. But you need to take care of yourself from now on, for the children's sake."

She hung up after he promised to change his ways. He didn't think he would, however; already he'd reduced the incident in his mind down to one of those "inevitable collapses" sedentary and overworked salaried employees were so prone to. He told his wife that he'd have to be more careful when playing with the children, making it sound as though he'd been tumbling along with them when in fact he remembered very clearly that, when it'd happened, he had been standing still, and apart from them, thinking about something else.

To her and to himself he said he had overexerted himself; at forty-one, he was getting too old to roughhouse. In a more serious discussion about the experience he described his lifelong issues with dizziness and his wife, upon hearing this, was comforted. She knew all about that; she'd been nauseous and weak all nine months carrying the girl. The boy had given her no trouble, but she recalled her pregnancies the way she thought back on her worst food-borne illnesses, as crucibles that had etched deep lines around her small mouth and altered her appetite so severely she would never eat anything even subtly tasting or smelling warmed-over ever again.

At home, he tried to relax while his family watched a movie together on the sofa (only the cat sat apart from them, for the deluxe massage chair belonged to him alone), but he noticed how frequently the children kept glancing his way, checking on him, it seemed to him. He wondered if they'd grown apprehensive about death—his own, and generally. Or, he thought, it was *he* who was feeling that way; the children were, he decided, just glad to have him back. He knew from experience that even going a day without someone you were used to seeing all the time could refresh your attitudes toward them. He recalled from his childhood how often he'd stayed up nights, waiting on his drunkard father; even as a boy of twelve, thirteen, he'd cried himself to sleep whenever the old man failed to find his way home after yet another bender.

A couple of days passed, and nothing else happened. Whatever they'd given him during his hospital stay, along with his mother-in-law's antler things, which arrived on Monday, were either placebos or they really did improve his general sense of vitality; so Gitae went back to his normal routine. He worked; his wife worked; the children went to school and their lessons.

Then one day, the apartment looked different to him—felt, for just a single moment, the way hotel rooms and vacation rental homes did when he was first settling into one. Its odors and upholstery and even the handles of the kitchen faucet were unfamiliar to him; he ran a hand across the warm glass of the veranda windows, touched the light switches on and off. Again he was struck by the disorienting sensation of stepping into a new place for the first time; nothing he touched felt old or worn or smelled like something that belonged to him.

Only the animals felt like home, like family. The cat and dog followed him as he went from room to room, as he looked, smelled, sensed. Then the moment passed, and the apartment slowly felt like his again. The strangeness of his home left his thoughts.

Later, he remarked on the episode to his wife, who explained to him that, unlike herself or even the children, he found the apartment unfamiliar because he was hardly in it; she told him he treated it like a second home, an officetel he didn't want to be in unless absolutely necessary. He worked too much and too long, she said, and he spent more hours alone in his office at work than anywhere else in the world. It was true: some weeks that summer he worked six days a week, coming home long after the children had been put to bed; he saw them in the mornings, Saturday evenings, and only partly on Sundays (the kids had English camp after morning service). He was due a mini vacation in August but, without consulting his wife, he'd opted out. The company would give him a double bonus at the end of the year in exchange. They didn't *need* more money, not right then ... but of course they always needed *more* money, particularly as the children grew older and would need to be enrolled at the better schools, either right in the city or, as his wife sometimes talked about, at one of the new alternative programs farther away. He wasn't after another promotion (he had no ambitions for anything higher than a team lead), but he sensed that putting in more hours during the slow season might lead to something better next year, when the company established its second campus in Seongnam. It was all for the sake of his family, he told himself, and when his wife managed the extra funds and benefits in the years to come, she would see his growing distance from his family as something he had most definitely been required to offer as sacrifice.

At breakfast the next morning the children were busy talking to each other about something they'd seen on television or perhaps had read in a book together, something rather incoherent to his ears; it was difficult to follow their conversation. Gitae was restless. The kitchen didn't entice him to linger there and have his coffee as the usual family noises filled the apartment. He stayed by the foyer with the dog, who was waiting patiently for his morning walk. The children were packed and readied for school. "Now, say goodbye to your father," his wife said, helping them into their rain boots. At the door they shouted their goodbyes over their little shoulders as they stepped delicately into their rain boots. He wanted to walk the kids at least as far down as the curb but his wife, fussing with their umbrellas at the door, blocked his way.

She sent the kids out, then turned back to leash the dog.

"I'll take him," he said.

"Don't bother. You need to get ready for work."

"I have time!"

"You don't," she said mysteriously as she went out the door with the dog.

Later that evening, when they were in bed, his wife said suddenly that she understood that he worked for their sake, not his. He knew then that she, too, had been thinking about their—very small—spat that morning. "It's the same with you men," she said. "I didn't even know what my father did for a living until I was about twenty-two. I can't even say I would've preferred him more at home. It would've been different, though. For my mom—for all of us. Anyway, I understand," she finished.

He was touched; he was very sleepy. At work he'd submitted emergency permits all day in advance of tomorrow's deadline, and hadn't even had time to take lunch. His cold shower had been invigorating, but now, with the air from the AC drying his hair, he fought off sleep.

"It was the same with your father, wasn't it?" his wife asked.

"What was?"

"Working—'work is all he *wants* to know,' my mother used to say about Dad, and I didn't understand what she was talking about at the time. I do now."

"Hmm," Gitae said. The dog and cat were asleep between them. When he absently stroked their backs they repositioned themselves so they could sleep together in peace, out of his reach.

No matter what his wife thought about it, Gitae knew he was an involved father because he knew his own feelings: he was interested and invested in his children. At work, regardless of how busy he was, he stopped what he was doing whenever the children's pre-school and Kindergarten teachers sent over alerts or messages. One afternoon, he received the usual assortment of photos and video clips of the kids their schools sent over to the group chats he and his wife took part in for this purpose. That day, the kids had gone on a joint field trip to the royal tombs—something he hadn't realized until he was looking through the photos. Though it was a busy day at work because of another team's minor screw-ups with a major client, Gitae shut the door to his office and carefully studied the kids' lunches, their plein-air watercolors, their group picture. No one looked much happy in this last photograph, his daughter in particular; one child, a boy Gitae didn't recognize, was standing beside her, his head turned to her when the photo was taken. For some reason it gave him the creeps, the kid in profile. The child looked angry, though Gitae didn't know why he should think so. He wondered if the kid had been yelling at his daughter.

A few hours later he was on the road, on his way home. As usual for that part of the city at half past seven, he sat in traffic; while he waited he played Matgo on his phone. In the middle of a frenzied animated sequence celebrating his AI opponent's outrageously fantastic draw, his wife called to tell him she was taking the children to see the fireworks at the closing ceremony of that year's neighborhood mask festival. "—came by," his wife said.

"Who?"

"So you'll have to take the dog out, I didn't have time," his wife said.

"Who came by?" Gitae asked again.

His wife was breathless, distracted; she was speaking to someone—not the children, but to an adult. The other woman giggled.

He tried to tell his wife that he could, and wanted to, join them later but she wasn't listening. She talked too loudly into the phone, sounding as though her head was turned away from the screen. She disconnected mid-laugh.

About forty minutes later he was home. His wife had left the air-con on and the apartment was much too cold; he turned the temperature up to twenty-six (they'd agreed never to leave the LG on below twenty-two but it'd been left at an astonishing eighteen Celsius) and switched on all the lamps in the living room. The cat, clearly put off by the intense chill, had hidden himself somewhere; the dog followed him around morosely until Gitae finally whistled at him, signaling the beginning of a walk. "Give me a sec, will you?" he said and poured himself a glass of water. With his wife and kids out of the apartment, he wasn't sure what to do with himself. He wanted a shower, a hot meal, and to be in bed by ten o'clock. But the dog needed walking, and he wasn't sure, really, if he should wait for the kids to come home or if he should take care of dinner on his own. It was almost half past eight now, which meant it'd be an hour or more until he was back and washed and ready for bed—but by then the children would be home, or on their way back. Would his wife want his help with their washing up? Did she want dinner on the table, or would they eat before they came home? Many small—but devastating—disagreements had come about because of his lack of interest in resolving that kind of dilemma. He tried calling his wife but it went straight to voicemail; he sent her two text messages inquiring about dinner, wording them carefully so she wouldn't think he was asking what was *she* going to do about *his* dinner.

The night was too warm to enjoy the air, but out on their walk the dog looked happy, even doing a little shimmy when he approached a pretty girl or a good tree. Gitae had no specific thoughts, only a vague sort of upset feeling. He wondered if he wasn't coming down with something again. He thought everything might change once his wife called, but she didn't, and he and the dog went farther and farther out.

Banners advertising the traditional mask festival had been hung up on every other streetlight; though it was a muggy, ugly night, families and couples crowded the streets; they all seemed to be heading in the same direction.

While crossing an intersection Gitae smelled a sort of old country smell, a combination of odors indescribable to city people like his wife but distinct and deeply pleasant to his mind. It made him think about his folks. Memories of his mother still wounded him, mostly because he remembered the way his father had been with her, the terrible things he saw and heard as a child. Like many drunks, his father had been an odd and troubled man who was loud and violent at home with his family but quiet and meek with outsiders. As the years passed Gitae remembered his father in isolation, in still, murky images. The clearest he could picture his father was of the old man sitting alone at the foldout table on the floor of their kitchen; that evening, on his walk, Gitae recalled another memory: of the old man making a mess of the scorched rice and spoiled side dishes that had been their supper once, when his mother had gone away from them for a time.

While the dog led him up a dark alley, seemingly in search of a private place where he could defecate, Gitae suddenly remembered how, one evening when his father had been drinking at the low table, he'd had gotten up in a rage. But instead of picking a fight or even turning the table over as Gitae had expected, his father had stood there swaying on his feet, spitting up like a baby, the stricken expression on his face unchanging. The boy Gitae had been had caught him by the armpits, and together they'd gone crashing down into the bottles.

He fingered his left elbow, feeling for the jagged band of thickened flesh running from funny bone almost to his wrist. He'd been a thin, pale boy growing up, on whom even a mosquito bite drew attention. Like his father, he was reticent, and he'd been naturally inclined toward telling the truth about himself because it cut conversations short. But when he was older his scar had required that he learn how to talk to people, to study them and tell them what needed to be said in order to satisfy them. With some of the nastier bullies the truth was found out eventually, whether he relinquished it or not; later he found it was far easier with girls and women, because some never even mentioned it while others only asked out of politeness, or because they sensed his apprehension. His wife had been one of the latter, but when he explained it away as a "childhood accident," she'd never asked him about it again.

The scar reminded Gitae of his recent collapse, which he hadn't stopped trying to figure out; he was more careful about how he walked now, the way he moved and sat and stood, how he felt in the mornings and his condition before bed. He was daily reminded of the weirdness of that whole incident. He knew it hadn't been a balancing issue, and he hadn't collapsed because of routine stress. He was supposed to go in for more tests but he'd been putting them off, using work as an excuse. There was something in the way it'd happened that was not only embarrassing but shameful to him somehow, galling because of its familiarity; he knew he was refusing to acknowledge something about his family history.

He'd thought about his father long enough, he decided, and called his dog back to him.

By the next block they reached what looked to be a staging area of the mask festival. The other pedestrians had scattered by now and Gitae could see no one beyond the barricades. The dog was tiring now, either because of the distance or the humidity, and because Gitae had no water with him, he guided his dog toward one of the apartment complexes down the street in search of a water fountain. They found one eventually, behind the waste bins; he fished a plastic container out of one of the recycling receptacles nearby and filled it to the top with warm, but perfectly drinkable, water. He set it down, then checked his phone again. His wife hadn't read her messages; her phone went again to voicemail. He wondered whether he should worry, but figured the fireworks were starting soon—he'd noted the time of the ceremony on the banners—and left her another message.

He'd come out with the dog, he said, in search of her and the kids. Could she pin her location for him?

The first of the fireworks went off. When it happened Gitae had been on the sidewalk, heading back toward the barricades. The leash hadn't been looped very loosely around his wrist, and the dog was old enough now to have mellowed out greatly from what he'd been as a one-, then a two-year-old Jindo. But the combination of noises from the fireworks and the distant crowd or perhaps due to some subtle change in the air, the dog startled and backed into Gitae's legs, his tail and sizable back end wagging uncertainly. Then the dog shot down the street. Gitae had enough sense to hold on to what he could, but he was pulled, hard, and took a wrong step into the grass. He let go of the leash.

Their dog wasn't the sort of dog to go running off because of a loud noise or some slack in his owner's grip. But he *had* gone.

Gitae walked down increasingly unfamiliar streets, regretting coming out of the apartment at all. To his mind, a man grew up to rely either on his two feet or his car, and he'd been a car man for the past twenty years; he'd limited his walks with the dog to the same ten or twelve blocks around their apartment complex. He hadn't been this far south in their neighborhood on foot, perhaps ever. The dog, no matter how intelligent and well-trained he was, was also in unfamiliar territory. They were two of a kind, couch potatoes with night blindness.

The streets grew narrower, and he was forced to turn down a side street due to construction on the main road. The doors to the buildings down this way were closed to him, with chained doors or steps leading down into dark and possibly uninhabited basements; the few shops he passed had shut down for the night. The pedestrians he saw now were men unlike himself; they were older men who moved slowly and with pained grimaces, as though ill. They walked right past him when he tried to ask them if they'd seen a dog down the other way. He called his wife again and again, left her panicked messages he typed in distractedly, with an eye on the street in case the dog came padding along. But he didn't. Gitae worried about fast cars, big rigs, and other dogs. The little bastard had come straight to them from a litter of two, and hadn't spent a single night outdoors. A sheltered dog like that might enjoy freedom at first, but only for a little while. He whistled for the dog, called out to him and waited. He heard nothing in return—no distant whine, no jangle of his collar and leash.

Gitae tried to remember if they'd registered the dog with the city, and thought it likely that they'd had him chipped—at least, he remembered telling his wife to take care of it. As with their children, his wife was responsible for that sort of thing. He'd never even taken the dog for his vaccinations.

It was nearly ten by the time he was home. He returned without the dog. And without a family: the apartment was dark when he got in.

He was tired, and soiled with sweat and dirt. He took a shower and, sitting on the couch in a damp towel, ordered for himself fish porridge through a delivery app; it came twenty minutes later, sealed in a plastic baggie inside a shallow compostable bowl. Though he normally liked porridges and stews, anything hot and spiced, what he squeezed out of the plastic rid him of any appetite he might've had: it looked like the slurry of something cooked in its own blood and brains.

He left it uneaten on the table and, remembering the cat hadn't yet welcomed him home, washed his bowls. Setting them out with fresh water and salmon paté didn't draw him out, but shaking a bag of treats did. The cat yawned as he came out of the children's bedroom, then sat in the middle of the living room, watching and waiting for Gitae, it seemed to him, to answer a very important question.

"I don't know either," Gitae said.

It was hours later, maybe. He opened his eyes and listened to the sounds of the kids putting away their things; then they were asking their mother something, their small, perhaps sleepy voices, overlapping; he heard her tell them to hurry in and wash up. He heard her go into the kitchen, presumably to cook something; upon seeing the uneaten porridge, maybe, his wife paused. She called out to the dog, then to Gitae.

He got up and realized it was only a quarter after eleven; he'd slept about ten minutes. He went into the kitchen, where his wife was rewashing the cat's bowls.

"I did that already," he said. "Why the hell didn't you answer your phone?"

She looked at him a moment, then seemed to understand something at the sight of his shirtless body, his wet hair. "I lost it," she said, turning back to the sink. "Can you believe that?"

He'd been preparing to blow up at her, but was now immediately spooked by the idea of some creep pawning her phone on the black market. "Where?"

"I don't know—one of the booths, maybe? I reported it to an employee, and she said they'd look into it for me."

Gitae relaxed, but made a mental note to remind his wife about suspending her cell service. He took a seat before explaining about the dog, in case it was her turn to unfairly blow up at him. His wife took it calmly; then he realized he'd mistaken her mild expression for indifference. She'd been thinking.

"We'll put the kids to bed, then go out and look for him."

"Is he chipped? Should we call someone?"

As he'd anticipated, she said she'd handle that. Could he check in on the kids for her, wash their hair and make sure to use the blow dryer, thoroughly, afterward? "Sure, sure," he said, relieved at the sight of his wife sprinting to her laptop, presumably to report their missing dog on the animal welfare center's website.

Short as it'd been, his nap had refreshed him. Gitae went into the bathroom ready to supervise the children's baths. He paused at the door. The boy had overdone it with the tear-free shampoo and his small dark head wore a strange second skin of bluish-green liquid; the girl had hidden her face behind all her black hair and for a moment, she appeared to be an eyeless, noseless thing with a sexless body, undulating like something that grew pale and squat in deep waters.

Gitae moved closer to get a better look; he turned on another overhead light, the one he used to shave, and the moment passed. The boy wiped the goo off his face, and grinned up at his father; the little girl, in rather a dog-like moment, shook herself from head down to her ankles, spraying strawberry-scented water everywhere.

"This is a lot of energy for eleven o'clock at night," Gitae said, rinsing off the boy's face. There was a rash or birthmark or something else on his son's left cheek, a little reddish crescent moon just under his eye. He left the boy to air dry while he helped rinse out his daughter's long black hair, then wrapped her in a big towel. When she hugged his neck he held him to her tightly, feeling more affection for her than he could remember since she'd been born. But when she pulled away and asked him where the dog was, Gitae noted the longer nose and slimmer cheeks, the way his little girl now held her head, slightly tilted to the side—it was modeled after their mother, he knew, but the gesture was new to her, and he found himself turning away from his daughter, as though he'd seen more of her than was appropriate, somehow.

As his wife put the children to bed Gitae got dressed to go out again. He heard her tell them their father had taken the dog to a special hospital that night after having come down with a rather happy case of dog flu, caused by special dancing ticks that lived in the long grass. The ticks were going to dance all night, and it was the humane thing to do, she said, to let them live in the dog's undercoat, just for the time being until they could be transferred safely elsewhere. Gitae went and stood at their door.

"That's not true," their little girl said, tilting her head at her mother without lifting it off her Cinnamoroll pillow.

"It is," his wife said. "Your father saw them dancing."

After a moment, his wife joined him, leaving the door to the children's room open so the cat could go in and out. She was always remembering to do that, while he only noticed he hadn't done it when the cat came and complained at him.

In the foyer Gitae got some of the dog's things out of the closet—his corn squeaky toy, a second leash—and put on his shoes.

"Why don't you stay with the kids?" he offered.

"Why? They're asleep."

"I'm the one who lost him."

His wife shrugged. "You said he ran off."

"That's practically the same thing."

"What if the kids wake up while we're gone?"

"They know better than to leave the apartment by themselves."

"Think of what'll happen if they do."

"Think of the alternative," his wife said. "They wake up in the morning and the dog's not home. They come home after school and the dog's still not home. Do you want to deal with that?"

They went out together, leaving a rather hostile-sounding note of warning on the door for the children and instructions to call their father if they needed anything. *Fifteen minutes, tops,* he thought. He'd been left alone for hours at his daughter's age, and once, for a whole night and part of the next day when his father had failed to come home after a drunken brawl. But in the car, as he drove round and round the neighborhood, Gitae wondered again about the kids. What if they'd woken up at the sound of the front door? What if they went out looking for the dog on their own?

He glanced over at his wife and found her uploading photos of the dog online; he fought the urge to comment about her choices. They were family photos, too revealing to post for the public even if his wife had blacked out their faces. Surely he had plenty of pictures of the dog posing alone? But they had only his cell phone and whatever he'd saved in the camera roll. He realized he couldn't remember taking any photos of the dog the way he had of the children, just him, facing the camera. The dog was part of the family, yes, but he wasn't important enough to be snapped for his own sake. The thought made him sad, and Gitae drove farther out in search of the poor bastard.

He parked the car near the festival barricades where he'd first stopped with the dog; his wife insisted on going beyond these, however, rather than circling back the way he had when the dog had gone off. It was past midnight, the air was terribly muggy, and he was only half-heartedly searching now. Gitae's mind was on the kids again; he didn't want to leave the children alone longer than he needed to. He figured they could search again in the morning—and besides, the animal control people would be able to locate the dog in no time, using his microchip information. He said so to his wife.

She looked away from him down an alley. They were almost entirely alone in this part of the neighborhood; on the road, only the occasional motorcycle went past, the odd taxi cab. His wife called the dog's name softly, so quietly no one could have heard her.

"Are you worried?" Gitae started to say, intending to ask about the kids. But his wife turned and smiled at him, her eyes searching the road beyond him.

"He'll turn up," she said.

Gitae relaxed; his wife was right. She was, he realized, a good wife and mother because she naturally knew and possessed much more than he did, and what she didn't know or have, she learned or pursued or found out. He thought about their kids, alone in the apartment. He remembered what it was like to wake in the dark to a cold house, how he'd gotten up to sit by the front door, waiting and watching for it to open. He couldn't remember now if he'd always known how to wait for his father to come home, or if his childhood had required that he learn to do it, with deep concentration, almost with pleasure, or at least to find in it a sort of comfort.

It wasn't comfortable now, the waiting. Every hot breeze and shadow and faint, suspicious sound forced him to relive the moment of the dog running off, recall the way he'd let go of the leash, as if he'd wanted to do it all along.

They walked past the barricades and across a deserted plaza. His wife went on ahead, telling him she had an idea of where the dog might have gone.

Seeing no one around, Gitae lit a cigarette and smoked it by a trash can. The area had been nicely cleaned up by the festival staff, but the occasional mask lay abandoned on the concrete and in the grass. He picked one up and dusted it off. The mask was a child's; it was no larger than his hand. He used it to fan himself, then when he heard his wife cry out and call to him, in terror or with terrible joy, sent it flying into the air.

Love Letters

I didn't dress up for the wedding. In fact, I hadn't even planned on going. Shortly after I received the invitation—by mass text, something that's always been personally offensive to me—I heard from my friend Sunyoung, who reached out to ask if I was attending, and how much was I planning on gifting the happy couple? She said she'd been laid off recently and couldn't afford much, and added that I should please refrain from any remarks about that, as she'd been perfectly miserable at her old job and was terribly okay about everything, for now; anyway, about the wedding money: Gunwoo would just have to understand. What was money between old friends?

I replied with an animated emoticon of two porcupines hugging. I admitted I'd been planning on sending Gunwoo a paltry two hundred, and not attending, which was practically like giving him double that much, as I wouldn't be taking up space at the reception. True, my friend said. After a few minutes, she texted back: *Two hundred thousand won? Really?*

Okay three, but that's, like, absolutely the maximum anyone would expect of us, I replied. I knew the number was closer, probably, to about five times that for "such close friends," but she made no immediate comment.

Over the next couple of days, Sunyoung and I agreed to RSVP and to a cool two fifty each. We even arranged to attend the wedding together. Neither of us had seen him in years and though we didn't say it, I think we were both more than a little put off by the invitation coming to us from out of the blue. We'd grown distant and I, for one, had no real idea, apart from messaging app profile photos and what could be gleaned online, of who the bride was or even, really, what sort of man he was aging into. I remembered Gunwoo as a good friend, at least during our middle school years. He'd been one of those good-humored, unathletic, sexually neutral (for a time) boys who can get along with just about anyone. But we weren't exceptionally close; it's unusual, I think, that Sunyoung, Gunwoo, and I kept in touch over the years, but all I can say about that is it was more accidental or even coincidental than anything. For some reason, after high school, we kept running into one another in some way or another; a friend I had would also be friends with Gunwoo or Sunyoung, and so on. More importantly, nothing had happened to make us sever ties with one another.

I wondered about how long that sort of thing would last as we moved out of our thirties and into our forties. I wondered, too, if his invitation had been accidental or deliberate. It seemed likely that, as the generically-worded mass text indicated to me, he'd simply wanted to fill his wedding purse and was fishing for congratulations. Despite my suspicions, I hoped the last few years had been good to Gunwoo.

The wedding reception was held at the C—Hotel, at two o'clock. Sunyoung picked me up in a little blue import; it was new. "Hey, gorgeous," she said. Her skin and hair looked new, too. I took a long time folding myself into the passenger seat because I was wearing a lot of layers and it was a windy day; I'd done nothing with my hair, and with every fresh breeze I wondered if my foundation was flaking. I hadn't dressed up and didn't do much with my looks, as a rule, but with Sunyoung so dolled up beside me, I wondered if I hadn't made a mistake. Not just on that afternoon, but with my whole life. My hand-me-down designer purse embarrassed me deeply; I'd almost instinctively set it down on the floor before Sunyoung caught me. She insisted that

I give it its own seat in the back, next to hers (a Bottega Veneta, she said, she'd gotten it to complement her dress for the wedding).

"Supplement shot," Sunyoung said, offering me a urine-yellow glutathione strip. I stuck it behind my front teeth on the roof of my mouth, as instructed. It gradually melted down into a sort of plaque I was forced to swallow or else have the taste of sour plastic in my mouth assaulting my tongue a minute longer.

"What's it do?" I asked.

"Hell if I know. I got five hundred of these off a home shopping deal. Take a couple boxes with you, will you?"

I stuffed a single twenty-strip pack into my purse and, while I was tucking it under my wallet, was freshly troubled by the money envelope containing three hundred thousand won (after another back-and-forth we'd increased our cash gifts back up to three) for Gunwoo. Despite our agreement, I was sure Sunyoung would be giving him two or three times that, if not more. Surely, in comparison, my money would come across as an insult, as cheapness. In my own affairs, cheapness saw me through; but I wished also not to offend.

Anyway, I thought, it was too late now to change my mind. I carried no extra cash and would have died rather than ask Sunyoung to stop at an ATM. She was quick and, even in our youth, had always read people accurately: she would've seen right through me.

I spent the rest of the drive looking ahead to my evening—when, six or seven hours later, I could be washed and in my pajamas, sitting up with a book and a nice big can of Stella Artois. I wasn't a total grouch, however; it was a busy, beautiful May morning, surely a good sign of things to come for the couple.

The reception looked just as I'd expected it to. Everything was very chic and strictly monochromatic, as was the trend these days. I haven't been to a single tasteless wedding this decade. In this city I don't think it's possible to really pay for or even to witness a truly bad one. The professionals you can hire, from caterer to florist, seem to know exactly what they're doing. I was sure *something* was going wrong here, behind the scenes, but as a guest I saw absolutely nothing amiss. Everything was just so: the emcee was semi-famous and witty; the staff was appropriately attentive; the food was fusion-Italian, heavy on the cream and only lightly seasoned. Beyond the main stage you could use one of three separate photo booths or even take a nap in the rest nook; there was also a separate video room, where you could record a message for the couple. On each of our tables we were assigned one of four different wedding favors—a voluptuous jar of French lavender honey, a His & Hers duo set of hand cream, luxury bath slippers, or a satchel of fancy fortune cookies.

I didn't mingle, but I spotted a few familiar faces. Sunyoung seemed to know the same four people I knew but it seemed pointless to sit or move together as there was plenty to do at our own table. After a while I journeyed alone to the restroom, where I found a separate mirrored area for ladies who wished to powder their noses. I spent a long time at the mirror pretending I was touching up my makeup. It was warm here, and relatively private. We were only halfway through but the reception was wearing me out. This was, I realized, the first time in a long while that I'd been surrounded by hundreds of people under the same roof. I was tired, and I'd strained my eyes trying to look so attentive. By the time I was heading back out, I realized a speech by the groom was underway and hurried back to my table, hoping not to catch anyone's eye. But not even Sunyoung seemed to have realized I'd been missing.

It was the usual sort of thing, Gunwoo's speech. Well-rehearsed, pleasant, not funny (though you had to laugh politely when he paused, expecting it), and unmemorable. He glowed under the lights in his cream tuxedo; he'd lost a little weight since I'd seen him last. His hair transplant, though obvious, looked good. I could also tell he'd done something with his face. His wife, meanwhile, stood rigidly beside him in her strapless gown. She smiled once, but even that looked forced. I was glad for Gunwoo. I sensed, based purely on what I could make of the woman and her collarbones, that the marriage was going to be a success.

As I watched the man on stage with his new bride, it brought to mind an important fact about Gunwoo and myself, something I hadn't thought about in years: I was, according to him, his first love. It was something I recalled without much emotion now, though long ago as a girl it used to make me squirm. I had no idea what'd happened to the love letters he used to write me, for I didn't think I'd returned them, and couldn't remember too much about what else had been written in them. None had been over a page long; vaguely I could still see them, those thin bluish sheets with their neat gray characters.

In middle and high school Gunwoo and I had been average students without older or younger siblings, which meant we shared friends between us and socially, we were well aware of each other. I don't know if I would have reacted differently if a boy I knew less familiarly had given me my first love confession. Possibly it might have given me more of a thrill.

Back then, I thought at first Gunwoo's strange behavior toward me was because he was in love with Sunyoung or one of my other friends; I assumed he was trying to get on my good side, so he could rely on me as a go-between. Even then I'd disliked doing favors for people, as I never asked them of others.

On the day of his initial confession of love to me we were outside the school gate, each about to turn and walk down the opposite street. It'd been a windy day, and cold, the smell of exhaust fumes from an idling truck poisoning the air. Immediately I'd sensed the wrongness in Gunwoo's voice and . . . in his orientation toward me. He stared; he stood too close.

When he pressed a folded-up piece of paper into my hands I assumed he wanted me to pass it on to a girlfriend. I was about to ask which one it was when suddenly he said: "Open it."

He looked very pleased with himself; I found his smugness more repellent than even his unwanted closeness.

I asked him what this was about; I was thinking about favors owed, a cheat sheet, shopping lists.

"It's for you," Gunwoo said. "I wrote it *for you.*"

"I didn't ask you to do *anything* for me."

"I know that, stupid."

"Then I don't need this, do I?"

"But you have to open it while I'm watching," Gunwoo insisted.

"Why?"

"I want to see your reaction. And I want your answer right away."

As an only child of busy, distracted parents, I'd never gotten into much trouble but I'd also never attracted much unwanted notice. That was why it'd been odd even to myself, my hostile reaction to Gunwoo's confession. His interest had been the first of its kind. I should have been flattered. Instead I'd been frightened, and for some reason, mortified.

Finally, exasperated, I read the letter aloud, holding it far away from myself, shielding my face with it from Gunwoo's watchful eyes:

"*I have been thinking about you for a long time,*" I spat. "*Do you think about me, too?*"

I handed it back to him.

"I don't get it," I said, walking away. I was trying to move very quickly, and Gunwoo sort of jogged beside me, looking agitated.

"What's so confusing?" he said. "*I like you!*"

We applauded as the couple cut into a four-tier cake, which was one of those intricately iced, for-display-only deals. The bride and groom fed each other nibbles of their one slice; then the servers brought out cups of tapioca pudding and melon balls. We were supposed to be delighted with our unpretentious desserts, I think. I wanted cake.

Sunyoung left early (some emergency with her new apartment flooring installation—she said she'd invite me over after the dust had settled). I hadn't wanted to stay for dessert, but I missed my chance to follow her out. I was always unlucky in little things like that; somehow, for whatever reason, I tended to attract notice when I shouldn't— theater ushers, for example, were always stopping me on my way to and from the restroom to check my ticket, and no matter how frequently I visited, the security guards posted in the lobby of my friend's luxury apartment complex asked to see my identification even though I recognized them and they were sure to remember me, or at least the number of the unit I was always coming round to visit, and was never allowed to bypass protocol. Sometimes I wonder if I look suspicious to certain people, like someone not to be trusted, a woman you don't just wave through, allow in, leave alone to do as she will.

I was sitting there eyeing the wedding favor Sunyoung had left behind when the happy couple broke away from their cake ceremony and what I recognized as the band's cue to begin mingling started up again. I'd just made up my mind to swipe her lavender honey (my seat had been assigned a satchel of the dry-looking fortune cookies) when Gunwoo and his bride approached our section for their final meet-and-greets.

It happened as if he'd planned it this way all along: Gunwoo spotted me sitting alone, my desserts eaten and my old purse agape in my lap, obvious to anyone looking that I was about to shamelessly swipe more than one wedding souvenir for myself. He shot me an immensely artificial smile and bounded my way. I could do nothing but tip my head at him, like an idiot, as though we were mere acquaintances.

It's always humiliating, waiting for someone like Gunwoo to make his way over to you. He was interrupted by four different guests who pulled him into four different conversations, though he did try to cut them short with lots of boisterous talk and pointed laughter. After each person he managed to get away from he shot me a look, holding me to my seat. I should have broken away and escaped, for there was no real reason for me to greet him personally, but I sat there, waiting for Gunwoo like a fool, resigned to the awkwardness of our conversation before it happened. What made things worse was I had no Sunyoung around, no third party to reliably diffuse the tension.

"There you are, my good friend," he said as if he hadn't been ignoring me throughout the reception. I knew he'd been avoiding looking our way while Sunyoung had still been here. We were probably his oldest acquaintances at the wedding and he hadn't made his way over to our table until now. It was a deliberate oversight—and pointlessly rude. I hadn't realized until this moment that the other three at our table must've been paid seat fillers, for none were approached by the bride and no one looked particularly interested in Gunwoo as he took Sunyoung's empty seat.

"Congratulations," I said, and though I didn't want to, gave his hand a small pat. He squeezed two of my fingers then hid his hands from me, placing them under the table.

"Hey, that means so much."

"You look good," I said. Up close his skin was awful. He was wearing too much makeup over what had obviously been some sort of reaction to injections or laser treatment. He'd seemed halfway attractive from afar. My mood lifted.

"You, too. You look healthy. No late nights for you, I see."

These were the kind of comments you'd expect from a catty aunt who didn't like you very much. I smiled gratefully at him. "You have a beautiful bride. Congratulations again."

"I'm so glad you came," Gunwoo said.

"Thanks for the invitation."

He tucked his chin into his hand; he waved at someone who must've been walking behind me.

"You just missed Sunyoung," I said. "She was here for most of the reception, but she had to leave early. She wishes you well."

Gunwoo nodded absently. "I'll give her a call."

"Friend," I said, leaning forward as I shut up my purse, "you have my best wishes. You'll be very happy together."

"You're not leaving already, are you?" he said, getting up with me. "We ought to take a picture together. I'll have them send it to you, framed, when it comes out."

I patted his arm. "It was good to see you." I said I'd called for a cab and had to hurry out to meet it.

"So cancel it," he said. "Soon I'll be too busy for my old friends. I know that. You know that. This might be the last time we get to see one another like this. Come on," he said. "I mean it about the photo. I won't take no for an answer. You know that about me. In fact, you probably know me better than anyone here." And then he gave me a wink.

After the first, Gunwoo waited two days before writing me another love letter. I took it unread to the girls' bathroom, where I buried it under a pile of used tissue paper and soiled maxi pads.

Gunwoo and I were in the same class but I found it easier than I imagined to avoid him that day. Sunyoung and I were part of a large friend group—six strong, without a single boy in the mix—and as none of us were academically inclined, we took only lunchtime and the rules of the cafeteria matrons seriously, which meant my friends wouldn't allow Gunwoo or the other boys to even pass looks over to our table. Our physical education hour, which followed the noon break, was much more dangerous; fortunately, we were assigned to individual stretching and light jogging for the period, so I spent as much time as I could in the shadow of my tallest friend, Guija, listening to her complaints about our uncharismatic history teacher, her chauvinist grandfather, her family's many dogs. Despite her loud voice and what could too often feel like one-sided conversations, she was also someone who could catch wind of gossip days before anyone else. Eventually her gaze slid over to where Gunwoo and his group were stretching in one corner of the athletic field.

"So what's the deal with you and him?" Guija asked.

"Who?"

"What 'Who'? You and Choi Gunwoo, that's who."

I was at first disturbed that Guija had caught on to what was happening to me so quickly, then incensed that perhaps he had already begun spreading rumors about us, despite my explicit rejection of his confession. Or had I been more opaque than I'd meant to be? Perhaps, I thought with horror, he was flattering himself by assuming I was simply playing hard to get. Maybe he thought I hadn't rejected him at all. I tried to think over our conversation from the day before but couldn't remember what I'd said to him, exactly, only how I felt.

"Are you a couple?" Guija pressed.

"Of course not," I said. "Can we start walking, please?" I glanced back and found Gunwoo watching us, his arm around a friend. At the sound of their laughter and impressed hoots, I quickly turned away.

"Bastard," I said.

"You think you know someone," Guija said, cracking her knuckles. "So you gotta explain the situation to me, sister. In your own words. Are you together or aren't you?"

"I'd rather eat one of your dogs' vomit. No offense."

"No problem," Guija said. She was rarely offended when something could be true, according to her many stories her dogs did vomit a worrying amount, and I never joked about the things I would or wouldn't put in my mouth for I was the pickiest eater in our friend group and refused, at the time, all cucumbers, leeks, bell peppers, tofu, most stews, pork, ripe persimmons (though they were fine dried), cheese, American and otherwise, and any sort of chocolate with nuts. This was considered by girls like Guija and Sunyoung to be among my finer qualities, for it meant their waiting chopsticks and rice bowls and hands were the beneficiaries of my weirdness about food; I gave away as much as forty percent of my lunch at any given time. "So what, he's got a crush on you or something?"

"I don't think of him that way at all."

"You know, if you like him, it's no problem with me."

"I told you, I don't think of him like that."

"Like what?"

You didn't really have to answer Guija's questions, only the ones you wanted to address, and she was okay with that. In that way she reminded me of my mother; they were outwardly generous people, but if you crossed some line of theirs that only they knew about they turned away from you, permanently.

"Like someone I could be attracted to," I said. "He gives me the creeps."

"What a problem to have," Guija said. "Let's go smoke in the phone booth."

There was an abandoned phone booth that had either been dumped or installed by the side of an unpaved road at the back of our school, which you could access through an unlatched gate behind the equipment shed. There was no real need for two or three girls to squeeze together into that phone booth to smoke, as there were plenty of spots along the road where you could escape the yard teacher's notice, but we always did.

"Gunwoo likes Yeonsu," Guija announced when Sunyoung slipped in behind us.

"He has no clue," Sunyoung said.

"What's that supposed to mean?"

"What'd he do, kiss you or something?"

Guija told her about the two letters, exaggerating their demise.

"Aw, you're no fun," Sunyoung said.

Guija had found a toothpick from somewhere and began digging out a blackhead using my compact mirror. "The second letter's probably still in the trash can."

"I flushed it," I said, squatting by the girls' feet. I played with a book of matches we kept hidden inside. I could never quite light a match, then or now; I've always hesitated at just the wrong moment, the moment of the initial strike.

"Let's go check," Sunyoung said.

"I told you, I flushed it."

"Then we won't find anything, right?"

We did find the letter, in the bathroom after school. We read it squeezed in together, the three of us, into the same stall. First Sunyoung read it, then Guija, then finally I had to admit I hadn't even read it in the first place. The girls decided we needed to discuss it more thoroughly that afternoon, off-campus, so we all decided to ditch our after-school academies to play hooky at Guija's cousin's hair salon. We planted ourselves in the back room and read the letter over and over again, running the forensics. At one point, after a fit of giggling at Gunwoo's expense, ravenous, we ordered black bean noodles— Guija's cousin treated us—and Sunyoung read the letter aloud again, affected, with an intense but zany scrutiny, like a speaker at a feminists' march, overemphasizing every other word. At first even I found it funny but by the end of her reading I was disturbed.

"He's a much bigger weirdo than we thought," Guija said. "He talks about you as if you were dirt until he decided he liked you."

I frowned. "Is that true?"

"Let me see that," Sunyoung said.

I looked at it over her shoulder, studying the penmanship again. As neat as it looked, I was also certain he'd dashed it off. I voiced this concern aloud but something on the radio just then reminded Guija of another story about one of her uncles and by the time she was through telling it the thing between me and Gunwoo was forgotten for the rest of the afternoon.

Over the next few days he gave me two more letters, which I accepted only so I could show Guija and Sunyoung and the other girls in our group. At first I thought Gunwoo would be upset at having been found out and gossiped about like this, but I discovered he was actually enjoying the attention. He pursued me openly now, buying me chocolates (without nuts) and little plastic jugs of flavored milk and other gifts; he even walked me home after school, when he could, though we were rarely alone together as we were often accompanied by friends of his, or mine. I realized something about Gunwoo's attachment to me, and fairly early on. His courtship made me uncomfortable because I knew what he was, and what he wasn't after. It was clear to me, and I think to everyone else, too, that he liked me only because of my very indifference to the discrepant social importance of stupid boys and their sexuality. He was never going to ask me to be his girlfriend.

About a month after the wedding, he sent me a package. I found it waiting by my front door when I got home from work.

It was what he'd promised: a framed photograph of the two of us at the reception, about the size and width of a gift box of pears. I still thought it an odd thing for a newlywed to send anyone, even if I was an old childhood friend. He looked good, generously airbrushed and resized to an odd, smooth, and smaller-headed version of the man he was now. I had been touched up less, but not because I hadn't needed it. I couldn't imagine Gunwoo putting in a special request to the photo people on my behalf. What it probably had been was slapdash work for Guest, extra care for Gunwoo.

I waited a couple of days, then texted him a clipped thank-you message. He didn't respond for weeks; and when he finally did, he invited me out for a drink. Ignoring my noncommittal reply, he chose a whiskey bar in his neighborhood although it'd be a considerable trek there (it was a fifteen-minute walk just to the bar from the station, and I'd have to transfer twice on the subway), then back, and on a weeknight. He set the time—eight thirty—then said his wife would expect him home by ten, tagging little multi-colored heart emojis by the word "wife." His messaging app profile photo was of him and his bride on a boat on an American lake, the sun setting behind them. Their honeymoon, I guessed. His wife had been captured mid-blink; she looked unwell, swollen from the long flight over, unrested. The photo clearly favored Gunwoo—a strangely cruel or careless choice for a newlywed's public profile.

I tried not to read too much into it. But once that sort of thing was apparent to me, I couldn't ignore it.

George

What made a long flight worse was the feeling that I alone was having such a hard time while everyone else had figured out how this was supposed to be done. Even the child sitting beside me had been perfectly behaved, sleeping when it grew dark and waking to eat or use the toilet when the lights came on again. Perhaps due to my staring, the boy stirred. He looked at me, studied me, it seemed to me, then closed his eyes again.

It was another hour before the other passengers began waking up. They spoke in soft voices of things they needed: water; light; more blankets or for these things to be taken away; the time. Window shades went up; men lined up for the toilet, women called for attendants. Soon I could smell it: breakfast—American sausage, hotcakes. The boy beside me sat up and put in his ear buds. He began watching a movie so I watched it with him—a series of strange, muddled pictures of underlit faces and stage sets I couldn't make sense of. I wondered if there wasn't something wrong with the screen, or if it was just another sign of the times: some of the newer things in this world weren't supposed to communicate anything meaningful to people of my generation.

The flight crew rolled out their trays of hot towels and breakfast. I tried not to make eye contact with the attendants until it was my turn to speak up for what I wanted, which I found uncomfortably awkward. Eventually, this passed, and a tray of food was presented to me; I received coffee, and, though the boy said something very similar to what I had just said, orange juice in a plastic cup was served to my neighbor. In my unwashed mouth the cheese tasted like spoiled figs and the pat of butter on my dry croissant stuck to my teeth like sour gum.

I'd forgotten what flying was like. It'd been tolerable for the first forty-five minutes, then my absolute distaste for this kind of thing had kicked in. For the rest of the trip I was too restless and uncomfortable to think properly about my second visit to America, and I still had reservations about why I was doing it. My brother didn't know I was coming. He was expecting a return phone call from me, not for me to show up at his door. This spur-of-the-moment vacation now meant I had no money for the spine-correction package I'd been eyeing for the past couple of months. There'd been a grace period of three days after I'd purchased the ticket through a travel agency during which I could have changed my mind. But I'd let them slip by.

I checked the flight's progress again and again until we were finally touching down in LAX at a little past five in the morning. The new suit I was wearing had been yet another mistake. All I had to show for it was a crick in my neck, and BO from sitting in a polyester shirt for twelve hours. I was self-conscious about bumping into the other passengers as they made their way off the plane and waited in my seat, pretending to be absorbed in a round of Matgo on my phone. The little boy at my side, I saw, had been seated away from his father, who, yawning, came up the aisle to join him.

All my distress and discomfort vanished as I moved down the sky bridge and through the shining tunnels of the airport. Shops appeared, but not as many as I was always anticipating in such places. Outside, the air felt warm and good in my hair and nostrils; the skies were wide and clear. Instantly I was in a better mood, though I didn't know yet where I should go next. I wasn't going to be staying with my brother in Los Angeles since he'd moved up north. He wasn't going to be put out at all by my visit, which was how I wanted things to be when I was ready to see him. I'd done the opposite of what I was doing now the first time I came to see America, relying on him for everything from the moment I came out of baggage claim until the day I left. I wanted to see him as my own man and take care of my own matters; I was even going to rent a car so I could drive up to see him, then make the drive back down to LA when I was ready to leave again.

Where I was standing, I noticed the brighter expressions belonged to the people waiting in line at one of the shuttle stops. I stood with them, nodding back at an old man in a blue Dodgers hat who nodded, smiling, at me.

I'd never taken public transport in America so I was worried, a little, about figuring out how I'd get on one of the buses that eventually came along. I couldn't make sense of it, how to pay the fare and what, even, the fare might be. Then one slowed to a stop before us, and the old man in the blue hat waved some papers at the driver, a large man in a black uniform who merely waved the man on board. So I waved *my* papers at the driver, who waved us all on board.

Just like the buses back home, the last passenger hadn't even found his seat before we were speeding away from the terminal. We moved down elevated roads that looped the terminals, then we were out in the city proper where we jostled for position in bumper-to-bumper traffic. We went through no scenic routes and once we hit another freeway it seemed there was nothing worth studying but the passengers around me looked gravely and anxiously out of their windows as if relaxing in their seats meant something else when it was done on an airport shuttle rather than on a plane.

Perhaps an hour later we were moving through LA. I thought I recognized certain sights and shops, the look of the street signs. But it was hard to tell what was remembered and which had been shots I recalled from the movies. For long stretches there was nothing I wanted to pay attention to. We passed no landmarks, nothing I was going to want to see.

The bus dropped us off downtown. I took up my place among the people on the street, wondering which direction opened out to the better hotels. I passed a number of turn-of-the-century buildings; in front of these was always a handful of people stopped right in the middle of the sidewalk, forcing me to move carefully around their many large and soiled-looking carriers or else squeeze my way past their lumpy, greasy backpacks. In front of one hotel called the Ambassador were two people arguing in what sounded like a sort of made-up gibberish; they pointed at each other, then gestured at a hotel across the way, which announced itself as "Aspire." When they noticed my staring, I hurriedly moved away from them and turned toward the nearest hotel.

At the door I was assisted by a bottom-heavy Latino doorman who tipped his head and welcomed me warmly. I reached into my wallet and carelessly retrieved a bill which passed from my hand to his and then vanished into the doorman's coat. "Appreciated," he said mildly.

Inside, the hotel was various shades of maroon and soft pink carpet; it was underlit and furnished like an old-fashioned steakhouse.

"A single for you, sir?" was the first question from the woman at the front desk. When I answered, her fingers did a sort of square dance around the keys. "Last one we have with a tub instead of a shower is on the third floor, with an eastern view. Will that be one night or two?"

I put up a single finger, conserving my English in case I needed it later. I was paying for my room with my debit card when something about the look of the black plastic reminded me of something—

—my luggage. I'd forgotten it back at the airport.

"Yes?" the woman said, smiling very warmly at me.

I turned one back on her, recalling the lean and unhappy face of my old conversational English instructor. He'd made us drill exactly these kinds of situations until we could check in and out at any anglophone hotel desk in our sleep. "May I ask a favor?" I asked carefully.

While I was waiting for my luggage to arrive I took a bath. I had given the hotel staff as much information about my carrier as I could, though I hadn't been sure if the woman at the desk could help me, exactly, despite her warm assurances that she would "try everything" she could; I wondered if there'd be some trouble retrieving it, even if the man the hotel sent over was clever enough to pose as myself. I'd handed my ID over to the desk, just in case.

A few hours later it was quietly delivered to my door by a soft-spoken, middle-aged South Asian man, who, with his dark hair and eyes, might pass for anyone. Without being asked he rolled my carrier into the suite closet where he expertly rolled it on its side, leaving it ready to be opened. He reinserted the handle, dusted off the wheels with a handkerchief that appeared and disappeared into his pocket, then tipped his head at me and stood with his hands behind his back.

"For you," I said, and moved two beautiful American bills into his line of vision.

He didn't overstay his welcome; after a nice sticky nod at me, the man went out and shut the door softly after himself.

During my bath I'd been at a loss trying to understand my own absentmindedness. My luggage had completely slipped my mind. I'd brought many important things in my carrier, in fact, every single item to be found within was something I'd agonized over back in Seoul. These were mostly gifts for my brother and his wife, and also some things for their new baby. I'd also brought the old family album, the only one in existence as far as I knew. That sort of thing belonged to my brother's family now; I had no use for it.

Some years ago my brother had moved out of Koreatown to take over a water store up in Bakersfield; within weeks of his arrival, he found a wife. If things had gone differently for him up there, I would have stayed in Seoul and been done with him the rest of my life. My brother had let his student visa expire in '02 and couldn't travel abroad if he wanted to stay in the country undetected. We would have been estranged for another decade, maybe. But the woman he'd found was a U.S. citizen, and soon, he'd told me, he was going to be one too. He seemed to have forgotten that I could have flown out to visit him whenever *I* wanted. But as the elder he seemed to view that sort of thing much differently than I did.

The last time we spoke, my brother told me his water store business was doing so well, he was opening two more. His wife was Korean Chinese, and young enough that she was expecting a child. It spun my head, one of us siring an American. And now my brother was rich, too.

"I'm going to sponsor you," he'd said on the phone. "You can live here and manage one of my stores, or all of them. Whatever you want."

I'd never told or asked of him anything that would've encouraged this sort of offer. I didn't know what my brother thought of the life I had made for myself, but it angered me, his insinuation that I had been waiting for just such an opportunity, as though he'd been struggling in California for two livelihoods, and not just his own.

In all the years my brother had been living in Los Angeles, I'd never thought to tell him to come home. And despite the lows of my twenties, he'd never invited me to stay with him in California even after I'd come out to visit him once, back when I was thirty-one and wanted to see America. It hadn't been a good trip.

Now he wanted me by his side. Not to repay me, and not because we missed each other. We spoke on the phone maybe once or twice a year, on our father's birthday and on our mother's, when he remembered it. If, as he claimed, he hadn't suddenly become a rich and happy man, I knew nothing would have changed between us. I'd always assumed that when one of us died we would finally deal with our decades-long separation, the way it'd been for my father and me. I'd planned on retrieving my brother's body, or his bones, whatever was left to me when he died alone in America; if I perished first, I expected to be buried by one of the hospital morgues tasked by the city with the disposal of paupers' remains. But I could see now that it was going to be different. My brother's new family ensured a much happier end for him, and probably a longer life. Whatever was going to happen to me in my old age was still going to happen, but now my brother, at least, was going to be mourned by his people.

I got a night's rest in the hotel room, helped along by the melatonin I'd packed in my carrier. While I was checking out the next morning, I asked the helpful woman at the desk for information about cell phones and a car rental place, and was connected to both within the hour. I put my things into the rental, which was almost exactly like the car I drove back home, and while I was in it, I stopped at a 76 in Koreatown to top up the tank. While I was waiting I called my brother using my new cell phone. At first he spoke carefully, sounding, to my ear, the way I did when I spoke English to strangers whose assistance I needed in some way.

"Hello, yeah," he said.

For some reason I didn't say anything right away, I just listened.

"Hello?" he said. "Who's this?"

"I'm coming to see you," I said carefully, disguising my voice.

"Who's this?" my brother said again.

It was different when my brother was calling me from overseas. Even before he had his water store and the wife and child he'd never called without sounding as though he was put out by the effort he was making for me, as if it embarrassed and troubled him to listen to the sound of my voice. Our conversations had never gone on longer than ten minutes. Sometimes even half that.

I'd almost wanted to hang up on him when he'd called that day, when he'd spoken to me in that bluffing, booming voice he used when he was feeling emotional about something. He'd claimed his life in California was shaping into something he wanted to share with me.

I cleared my throat. "Give me the address of your water store in Bakersfield."

He paused, possibly recognizing my voice. I hoped he thought I was some enterprising vendor or customer with a weird accent, another Korean, but not one like him. It was the suspicion and appraisal in his voice that revealed everything he wasn't going to tell me about what he'd been through in this country. I sensed it was the way he always had to be in America, where he used to live alone.

I addressed him by the name he'd given himself out here, George. He let out a sound of relief or understanding, chuckling as though it meant something else to him.

"We're at 2020 Fair Oaks. Can't forget it, it's too easy to remember."

I laughed, tears in my eyes. "I hope not," I said.

What's So Funny?

What started it all happened on a weeknight; his wife had just cleared the dinner table. The dishes were washed and put away, the curtains were drawn, and a scented candle was lit to coat the odor of fried fish with a cloying idea of gardenias, raindrops.

Later, when it was all finished between them, Hyungsuk told everyone he knew that he'd divorced his wife because they were simply incompatible, which wasn't entirely a lie; he knew they were two very different individuals who'd stayed together as long as they did because they believed it was better to live with someone than it was to live alone. Also, they'd been told by enough people that they belonged together and it was nicer to believe that sort of thing than to try to work out the truth, which was that they were just like anybody else, neither perfectly suited for another human being, and not deserving of total deprivation.

When they split, they'd been at an age where their conflicts and disagreements were no longer about smoothing out differences in order to build a future together; they both knew there was no future for them. They joked less because they found different things tragic, and couldn't discuss politics at all as they belonged to different parties. They regularly and passionately voted against each other's interests.

That evening a typhoon warning was issued and everyone sensible stayed indoors. Hyungsuk stepped out for ten minutes to smoke two cigarettes in the shelter of the waste disposal hut near the playground.

He didn't feel anything amiss until the second he finished his second cigarette, when suddenly he saw, really saw, for the first time in a long while, the beautiful darkness of a late evening gone quiet and somber in the calm before a storm. Nature had a way of surprising him from time to time, something that never happened to him now when it came to people, or the daily routine of his life because there was so little of the actual world to be seen on his daily commutes to and from work in the city. Darkness and a strong wind had a way of making him romantic about things, or at least allowed him to notice things more profoundly and carefully—he thought it was that, maybe, that had something to do with what happened later.

Hyungsuk took the stairs back up to their apartment, where he found his wife as she usually was in the evenings: spread out on the sofa before the television, her face eclipsed by her very large phone, her feet up on the armrest. He went in and washed his hands, then sat next to his wife. He laughed along with the studio audience almost immediately; he'd just caught the tail end of a good gag.

His wife chuckled, too. She was still on her phone but she must've been listening, because she laughed right when the variety show's resident buffoon let out a pitiful wail after being shoved—playfully—against a padded wall by the older, superior comedian. Hyungsuk, who was a big fan of the buffoon, said, "That guy's always getting it." The younger man waited until the older comedian's back was turned, then gestured in a pleading motion to members of the production staff, who were waiting off camera. "This is not right," he said, his eyes as wide as he could make them. "Stop smiling, please! You know this isn't right!" The staff burst into laughter; the other cameras swiveled to capture them as they covered their faces with their hands, cowering behind cue cards.

Hyungsuk laughed, and thought to himself how pitiful his life was: he couldn't remember the last time he'd enjoyed himself so much. On TV, the older comedian extended the crew's laughter by hamming it up for the cameras, shaking his head with exaggerated disappointment.

That was when Hyungsuk heard it, a strange and unfamiliar voice, saying something softly, but distinctly to him: *"But you're lying. You enjoy yourself very much, don't you?"*

He was immediately chilled, for it'd been a woman's voice, though not his wife's, and sourced from someone or something sitting very, very close.

He looked over at his wife. She was sitting up now and giving the variety show her full attention. She looked perfectly normal; there was nothing about her, physically, that alarmed or disturbed him. Her face was still her face; she was still his wife. She turned up the volume on the TV and didn't seem to notice he was staring at her.

"What a pair of morons!" his wife said at the television, chuckling.

Hyungsuk did not, could not, stop looking at her. He studied her for some sign that she was pulling his leg; he waited for a hint of a sly smile to curl her lips, for her to break first. She wasn't the type to prank him, or to find that sort of thing funny, but he expected he didn't know her as well as he would've liked. She was always on her phone, for one thing, scrolling through hundreds of video clips a night. She might now be the sort of woman who found humor or pleasure in practical jokes; she might now be anyone at all.

The show ended, and his wife got up to brush her teeth. As usual, she took her phone with her. After a moment, he heard the tinny audio of what sounded like an instructional video for guided meditation.

Hyungsuk sat in front of the TV, which he shut off so he could think. He wondered if his wife's phone had been left on; perhaps one of her videos had been playing with the screen off? That sort of thing happened all the time. Only the theory dissatisfied him because of how *close* the voice had sounded, how it'd been most decidedly at ear-level. The voice had very definitely come at him from his *right* side, from where his wife had been sitting . . .

So of course there had to be another explanation, he thought.

He could have heard an errant bit of conversation from the upstairs or downstairs neighbor, or by a pedestrian out on the street. The sound could have been carried into their eleventh-floor apartment on the wind, which was at that very moment rattling their balcony windows. Or he could, he thought, just be hearing things.

But he hadn't. He'd never questioned his sanity or his physiological health before, and it felt foolish to him to make a pretense of it now just so he could tell himself he'd checked out every possibility. He *knew* he wasn't crazy; he was perfectly healthy, reasonable, and sane. The fact was, he'd heard something unusual: a strange voice had spoken to him in response to something he'd only been *thinking* about. It hadn't sounded like his wife, but then again, his wife could've been disguising her voice. Perhaps she was learning how to throw her voice from videos on the internet? She learned how to do everything else on it—she'd taught herself yoga stretches, (severely limited) conversational Japanese, and how to do her eyebrows better so she didn't look so angry all the time. Yes, he told himself, his wife was learning how to be a vaudevillian act, and was using him to practice. That was so much more believable, wasn't it, than the possibility that his wife was just fucking with him? But that wasn't why he was so chilled, was it? It wasn't the *voice* so much as it was what it'd *said*. He'd felt sorry for himself, and the voice had mocked him for it.

As he sat there, sweating, forcing himself to remain upright, feet planted firmly on the floor, hands sedately folded on his lap, he tried to make sense of what it all meant.

He was so focused on his thoughts and theories and calculations that he didn't hear his wife come out of the bathroom. He must've frightened her, he thought later. What a picture he would've made, sitting with his hands folded neatly before him, staring at the black screen of a cold TV.

His wife shook him ungently, which made him cry out in terror.

"What's wrong with you?" she screamed, because his wife raised her voice only when the other person did it first.

He got to his feet and scanned her from head to toe, ready to fight.

She was, as usual, more irritated than intrigued by anything out of the ordinary she detected in her husband. "What?" she said, flashing her black eyes at him. "*What are you looking at?*"

Hyungsuk stayed out in the living room late into the night, pretending to read a library copy of a book written by a little French boy who claimed to be the reincarnation of Nostradamus. It was the only way he could get his wife to leave him alone and stop nagging him about coming to bed. She assumed his work required that he keep his nose in nonfiction books, and, true to the conditions of their passionless marriage, his wife never seemed to question the titles of said books, even when they were clearly garbage without any relevance whatsoever for an employee in the accounting department of a safety manual publishing company.

As the hours passed, Hyungsuk had to admit to himself that he knew the truth. He decided his wife had to have spoken. It raised too many disturbing questions, but he felt it to be the only reasonable explanation.

He could no longer stay awake, and felt it was as good a time as any to finally turn in. But he only got as far as the bedroom door. There was something unnatural about the expression on his wife's "sleeping" face, a sort of firmness about the mouth that told him she was awake, and that in fact she'd been waiting for him, and had been on the verge of laughter when he'd shown up at the door. It confused and chilled him all over again.

At breakfast the next morning, he told his wife straight out what he believed had happened the night before.

"What the hell are you talking about?" she said, though he'd made himself perfectly clear. So he repeated himself, his bleary eyes fixed on hers (he'd slept only an hour, and that on the sofa, and that only in shallow fits of deeply troubled half-consciousness).

"Someone said something to me," he said, gritting his teeth, and repeated the words back to her. They embarrassed him; he was ashamed, mortified. He was always feeling sorry for himself; and yes, he had to admit he did enjoy a rather pleasant life. He worked a lot, of course, but so did his wife. And he could have been happier, and have more money, but that was true of most people. It was the sort of thing that might have happened to him as a boy of thirteen or fourteen, and often had. In a fit of restlessness or boredom he'd often lashed out at his mother, and she'd had to set him straight about all she did for him, all her sacrifices and toil, et cetera, remind him again and again of all that his poor dead father would have done and wanted for him.

"I do enjoy myself from time to time," Hyungsuk said quietly. "It's true. You got me there."

"I have no idea what you're talking about."

"Come on," Hyungsuk said, smiling. "*Come on.* Enough jokes."

His wife's expression changed, and she sat back. "Maybe what you heard was actually the TV. One of those new comedians, Popsicle, he's got a funny high-pitched voice like a woman. Maybe you misheard him?"

"No," he explained carefully, "*Popsicle* doesn't sound anything like a *woman.*"

"I don't agree."

She declared that she'd heard nothing unusual, nothing at all. She didn't have the faintest idea of what this was about. And frankly, she said, he was scaring her.

"Scaring *you!*" he said.

His wife grew irritated. Angry, even. She slipped on her apple-leather loafers and took up her summer-season handbag, a pale blue Prada, and whipped out the front door.

Of course, the last thing he wanted to do was follow her out; of course, he had to go to work.

So, he went to work.

Almost nine hours later, at two minutes past six o'clock, he was on the subway heading home, anxiously scrolling through a webtoon he wasn't reading. He continued to build his case with his suspicions, as well as with the facts. But as there were actually very few details to consider over and over (there was just the single event, the voice, and after a while he stopped being able to think about it all very clearly), he instead re-examined his wife's character and nature and attitudes, judging her against the standards to which he held himself, standards which he'd never before really articulated to himself, standards which seemed to him all-important now and totally at odds with the sort of woman he (now) knew his wife to be.

He worked backwards, beginning with the evening in question. It was easier to think about dinner: the fish she'd fried had been big and ugly and full of deadly little bones, necessitating quite a bit of time picking them all out; the stew, of course, had been bland, as usual; he'd found the potato side dish underwhelming (and under-cooked); and the rice had been gummy. His wife's character could most clearly be understood by the quality of the meals she set out. He (now) understood her to be lazy and sneaky, thoughtless, selfish, careless, and stupid. She prioritized and attended only to her imme-diate needs, her comfort. And what was more, she couldn't be trusted to be aware of the important things in life. A normal person with even the slightest interest in his well-being would have been more alarmed by his strange experience. His wife should have asked more questions, demanded more evidence. She should have been spooked, he real-ized, or at least intrigued. She should have, he thought later, come up with some theories of her own.

At work, he'd learned about something people called "locked-screen auditory leakage" on the internet, a phenomenon in which a seemingly "quiet" cell phone with its screen turned off or left charging could play an app in the background. With the way cell phones were nowadays, Hyungsuk figured they were even "smart" enough to pick up something he'd only mouthed. It was possible, he thought, that he'd said something under his breath, and, listening, his wife's idle phone had pulled up an audio clip in response. He was over forty now, and his hearing was probably only half as good as it could've been; maybe it'd just *sounded* close and he couldn't tell the difference, because he didn't know any better. Hell, maybe his own cell phone, which he'd left charging on his desk near the sofa, had actually done the "talking," and he'd assumed it'd come from the wrong direction.

Rather than feeling vindicated, he only felt sorrier for himself as he soothed himself with more evidence for the leakage theory. He knew now that it didn't matter what was true and what hadn't happened; what really mattered was that his wife didn't give a shit, and couldn't even perform giving a shit to spare his feelings. There was, he realized, truly nothing left between them.

Before this happened to him, his friends' relationship problems had always seemed to him matters of little consequence. He now recalled their reported issues of sexual incompatibility, of frigidness and profligacy and spats with in-laws, with horror: his friends' wives were spendthrifts, cold bitches, and idiots. *Why go on enduring them?* he thought. He couldn't imagine going out with a buddy to discuss how it was for him, living with a woman who cared so little about his existence that even entertaining an odd conversation about a funny little incident was beneath her. Talking about it wouldn't help him, he knew. He was *done*.

So for some weeks the matter simply remained unresolved and *just there* between Hyungsuk and his wife. She went on living her life, and he, studying her with growing resentment, lived his.

He awkwardly avoided his wife's eyes whenever he could, and disliked even walking too closely by her, feeling the little breeze as the edge of her shirt or wisp of her long hair brushed his arm. Each morning and evening that passed uneventfully between him and his wife gave him no peace, for he spent his free time anxiously looking up divorce lawyers on incognito mode even on his own cell phone browser.

When he was finally prepared to put his twelve-year-old relationship to sleep, he wanted to talk about it with someone. There was no one he could talk to, of course, without word reaching his wife. So he went to his mother.

"Do you think I'm overreacting?" he asked, after he'd explained everything.

His mother shrugged and examined her cuticles. "That's not for me to say." She was a late convert to Christianity and overzealous as a result; she was pious and energetically involved in her church, eager to proselytize, and bitchy about it, which was why he and his wife only saw her once or twice a year.

"But the pastor might know," she said, after a moment. "He'll know the moment he sees you. He can look into your heart without your having to say a single word. It's relief, you want isn't it? Well, only our Lord can give you that—but our pastor can do the next best thing."

He told his wife nothing of his visit to his mother and her holy man, with whom, as it turned out, he had quite a nice chat. When Hyungsuk was home he mentioned, as casually as he could, that his mother had called to invite them to a church picnic that Sunday.

"We're atheists and we're not going," his wife snapped. She was reclining on the sofa as usual. She didn't move her gaze from her phone screen to speak to him, though he could tell she was upset. She sat up and crossed her bluish-white legs, then drew them up to her chest. She wasn't really scrolling down the screen, he saw, but only pretending to look at something.

Hyungsuk had taken to sitting at the computer desk every evening after dinner, pretending to learn Russian, and it was there that he sat during this conversation. He also kept a stack of library books nearby at all times, and flipped through one whenever he found his wife looking at him.

"I'm not asking you to convert," he said to his wife, keeping eye contact with an animation of a green pigeon. It was wearing a rather overlarge ushanka and its beak moved excitedly but absurdly out of sync with whatever it was saying in Russian.

"*You* go then," she said.

"You know why she's asking us to come. She wants to see us."

"So *you* go," she said. "She's *your* mother."

He didn't go; Sunday morning came and went. They spent it not at his mother's church, but at home, as usual. They had a late breakfast, indulging in overly sweet soufflé pancakes while watching reruns of the variety shows that had aired that week. Hyungsuk felt sick, and more than a little sorry for himself.

He'd found the best divorce lawyer (according to reviews on a dozen Naver blogs) he wanted to afford, and he'd already filed the paperwork with a broker for a brand-new officetel ten minutes (on foot) from work. When he was out of sight of his wife, he spent his free time online looking at Ikea and West Elm, he was undecided about his furniture, for his wife was the one with an interest in that sort of thing, and couldn't make up his mind about spending too much on decorating his new bachelor apartment, or nothing at all. He thought he might remarry in a year or two, because after his talk with his mother's pastor he thought it better to limit his time spent alone. He wanted someone completely different this time, someone younger, for a woman who wanted children, he knew, would be more motivated to stay close to her mother-in-law. He wasn't going to be picky about her face, or even her body. Anyone who loved him and wanted to dote on him, he decided, would do, someone who'd take an interest.

Hyungsuk told his wife that he was going out for cigarettes. At that she raised herself on her elbow and gave him a mysterious look. "Don't be long," she said.

The day was gray but windless and warm. Hyungsuk felt strange. He was calm, but knew what was coming. There'd been something about the look in his wife's eyes that morning, something about the tone of her voice, that told him she knew what he was planning. What he couldn't figure out was how she felt about a divorce, or even a separation. Was that what she'd wanted all along? Or would she pretend to be surprised, and hurt? There was no real cause he could put forth for their divorce, he knew; without infidelity or abuse, he had to make a case for his unhappiness and dissatisfaction, and hers. She had to agree to separate, in any case, and in order for that to happen, they needed to talk, openly and honestly.

That, he knew, was asking too much from such a woman.

He went out walking by the neighborhood park. He smoked an entire pack of cigarettes. He was lost in thought, lost; when his last cigarette had been smoked down to nothing between his lips, a large van pulled to a stop beside him. He was not very surprised when the side door slid open, revealing his mother with a fresh perm, wearing her Sunday best. She waved him forward.

"I'm sorry we couldn't make it," he said. "The wife—"

"I prayed for you this morning," his mother said, cutting him off, "and I was given the answer. We had to come to you." He was waved in, and had to clamber across his mother and an old man to reach the only free seat in the back row. Someone—his mother, perhaps—picked the cigarette out of his mouth and tossed it out the back window.

He knew before unlocking the door that the apartment would be empty. When he led his mother and the others inside, it was all exactly as he'd expected it to be. His wife had left the TV on the home shopping channel; the hosts were squealing in delight over grilled beef intestines sold in four vacuum-sealed packs for the cost of practically one delivery-app order. Servings, he thought, too large for a person living alone. But for a couple, or a family of three, it was a pretty good deal.

He called out for his wife. He looked for her in one room, then another.

Hyungsuk gestured for his mother's friends to sit while he prepared a tray using his wife's tea things. He wondered what a man in his situation was supposed to do.

When his mother gently guided him out of the kitchen, Hyungsuk went into the bedroom to phone his wife.

After the divorce, the last clear thing he remembered about that Sunday was looking into the closets. While he waited for his wife to pick up, he'd suddenly felt certain that she'd been playing him for a fool after all; she *had* been lying to him. That was the only reason, he thought as he opened the final closet door, why a grown woman should hide while her husband and mother-in-law came into her home, calling out her name.

Reunion

I knew I was looking at myself when the girl didn't notice I'd been staring at her and her two girlfriends from the moment I'd spotted them. I
went on studying her from my corner of the subway car. They were just
as I remembered us being back then. There was Mosquito in her black
vinyl boots, her big flat face glowing with youth; sitting between us
was Sparrow, pretty as ever; and there, on the far end, looking intently
into her face, was me. Because the three of us were still together and
had not yet been split up by our parents, I put us at around fourteen.
The schoolgirl I used to be then wasn't pretty, of course, but I saw now
what people meant when they talked about youth forgiving all flaws,
physical and otherwise. I finally understood why relatives, teachers,
neighbors, and even strangers had been so kind to me growing up,
why it'd been so easy to get away with everything.

She—I—was the most observant of the trio; she was the only
girl to turn her head at the sight of a young man in his early twenties.
She looked at him for only a second, but I knew in that single glimpse
she'd noted the clean, not stylish clothes, his natural and good features, his aloneness. At her friends she made a little gesture, and her
eyes flashed at them. At once Mosquito stopped running her mouth
and followed her gaze. I thought I saw some doubt only in Sparrow's
face. That surprised me, her hesitation.

They got off at the next stop. The girls followed the young man
up the stairs and I followed them all out onto the street. The city

was dark—I grew dizzy thinking about the time. Hadn't it been . . . ? Wasn't I . . . ?

I felt nauseous and cold, as though I was coming down with something. But following the girls, I knew exactly where we were headed. It was all coming back to me. The girls walked on; I followed.

The young man stopped at a McDonald's. We waited on the street until another customer had gone in after him.

"How much money do we have?" Sparrow asked. That was always the question I remembered us posing to each other. It'd worried me a great deal then, the replenishing of my pocket money so I could go out with the girls.

The girls dug out their wallets—it brought tears to my eyes to see the childish props they still toted around: Mosquito's neon-green coin purse, the big cherry patch sewn on Sparrow's. I recognized my old wallet, the little Snoopy one I'd carried around with me everywhere until suddenly one day it'd vanished.

They counted out their money, producing just sixteen thousand won between them.

I let out a whistle. "Look at us. Three gold spoons."

"That's enough, isn't it?" Mosquito said.

"Let's decide what we want to eat now," Sparrow said. "We don't want to quibble inside in front of everyone and embarrass ourselves." She was the most self-conscious of the three of us. I remember having resented her for it at the time but now, looking at her, looking at all three little girls, I understood: Sparrow, of the three of us, was the one who was always being looked at, the only one of us in danger of being smothered to death with too much attention. At home her parents wouldn't leave her alone. Vitamin injections and a special diet, herbal brews, and of course the best clinics and tutors their money could afford: all to amplify her already considerable beauty and intelligence. Sparrow's family had big hopes for her: a good university, possibly even abroad; a short-lived career in some public-facing position; and finally, marriage to someone wealthy and important. Though we were only in middle school, Mosquito and I already knew our days with Sparrow were numbered.

We decided on a single order of large fries; a soft drink would be an extravagance, because we needed our money for whatever happened next.

Inside the McDonald's was a young crowd—beautiful children from the local private high school, and better-dressed kids from the no-name art college on the hill. "There he is," Mosquito said, her gaze fixed on the young man we were following. He was sitting alone with a book, wearing headphones, his Discman whirring away on the table.

I knew where this was headed and where we were going but I felt a curious excitement too, felt it much more strongly than regret or even apprehension. It puzzled me, my giddiness, because I remembered everything now.

Soon we were on the move again. The girls went out of the restaurant and were back on the street, but only for a moment. The young man entered a convenience store; we went in after him. In no time at all Sparrow struck up a conversation. He was not overeager; he was exactly as we thought he'd be. He looked at her the way we all looked at her. He was captivated, charmed, curious, wary. I loitered in the next aisle, watching it all happen.

The young man was old enough to purchase alcohol. At their request, he bought three big bottles of beer, and a little plastic thing of vodka. He bought cigarettes, chips, and candy. He bought four bowls of instant noodles. While they ate, he told them he kept a room three blocks away. I knew that already but the girls were just discovering this, as they sat with him at one of the plastic tables outside of the convenience store.

He was only twenty but looked older because he'd lived a life like Mosquito's, which was to say, unstable, with little love in it and even less material comfort. He explained that he'd dropped out of high school three years ago. He said this without any self-consciousness, as if it'd been inevitable and perfectly tolerable for him, that sort of thing having been part of the natural progression of his life. It changed my mind about what would happen next, because I hadn't remembered him at all, I realized, accurately. I hadn't known about his dignity and his obvious intelligence, his patience, the kindness that set his expression differently than other boys his age.

He had nothing for them, he said, because he could see they'd wanted something from him. The girls told him they wanted him to show them the little room he kept. "That's all, huh?" he said. I could tell, but the girls couldn't, that the young man was ashamed about his room. But he was also a man, and being a man, he knew how special Sparrow was.

As we went along with him he changed. He was quieter, had gone back to his closed-off self. He was again the stranger he'd been less than an hour ago, when he was contentedly alone on his way home with his bookbag and his Discman. I understood his guardedness but of course the girls didn't. It was why they went around, looking to spoil someone's evening. They knew nothing about why they felt as they did, they didn't yet understand.

The young man lived on the seventh floor of an old gray building. He didn't bother with a complicated string of numbers for the keypad on his door—and he let us all see it too: *0007*. "It's a joke," he said. No one found it funny.

We were shown in.

Then we saw how his little life really was; too much was revealed by how tidily he kept it. In one corner of the unit was a high window I'd seen from the street, one that couldn't have let in much good light or clean air or too much of the sounds of birds and people and the city. There was no television inside, only a small radio and some CDs, not many. And instead of a proper desk he used a short foldout tray, which, while not in use, he kept against the wall. What served as a kitchenette was a single block of stained plastic that served as a counter on which was a portable gas burner, and on that was a single clean metal pot without a lid. Right beside the bathroom door was a small laundry rack on which his three pairs of socks and four pairs of grayish underwear were drying like thin fish under a halogen dome light. There was hardly room for us all when eventually the young man and Sparrow and I sat together on the floor, in a circle, with our black school bags at our ankles. Mosquito chose to stay standing, vigilant about the area around her feet as if she were afraid something might scurry out of the walls and crawl up her bare legs.

I knew what was going to happen next. I wanted to reach them, tell the girls what was going to happen to them, and with the boy they thought they'd caught using their wiles.

But we've always been ready, was the last, strange thought I remembered.

I was on the floor of a moving subway car. It was late and there were only three other passengers; they were pointedly not looking in my direction. I knew exactly what they were trying not to see: a fortyish woman in business attire, her knee-length skirt pushed up around her hips, heels kicked off. I smelled myself and knew I'd thrown up all over my blouse. I looked across the subway car and saw no girls, only a row of empty seats.

Father

That night we were having sea snails for dinner. My husband was on his way home. I knew he'd want a hot shower and a shave (one of his quirks—he always shaved at night), so I figured I had half an hour, more if he was still on the expressway. I was about to pull the top off the can when he called to say he could stop by the supermarket—did I need anything? "Oh, beer," I said. Soju, if he wanted.

"I'll be home by eight," he said, which told me it was going to be well past. "If you get hungry, don't wait on my account."

"That's no fun. Oh, by the way—make sure you get Guinness."

I left the kitchen and went out to sneak a cigarette in the recycling area behind the apartment complex. It was drizzling. Somewhere nearby, a cat had forgotten to secure shelter and was crying in the dark. I felt for it, but wasn't moved enough to try and help; strays broke my heart, but not because I wanted to take them all home or anything like that. It seemed to me they waited very patiently in search of very little—to be dry when it was wet out, to have a little food or warmth or shade or a safe, dark place to sleep, and to escape notice when they felt they were in danger. As if the cat knew just how much I devoted myself to my own creature comforts, he started up again. Before he could guilt me into taking him home, I ran back upstairs to our warm and lovely apartment.

My husband was showered, shaved, and toweling off his hair when I cracked the can open. I disliked tinned food, but whelk—and sometimes pineapple—was an exception. I was about to toss the empty can into our recycling basket when I saw it: a little gift bag Dohwan had left by his shoes in the foyer. It was unmarked so I was less curious about it than if it'd been dark orange or if *Dior* had been written on it somewhere.

It was still there, untouched, when Dohwan and I toasted with our glasses of beer.

"*Guinness sure hits the spot,*" I said, repeating an old joke between us. But Dohwan wasn't listening; he picked up his chopsticks, clacked them at the salad, and didn't eat.

"You okay?" I asked. I wondered if he'd had a bad day at work. Or maybe he wasn't in the mood for sea snail salad? I understood that sort of thing; I disliked even looking at *pictures* of crabs and lobsters, but could eat them just fine once someone else had pulled all their legs and claws off before serving them to me.

Later that night, however, I found Dohwan sitting up in the living room. I thought he'd been out there doing his stretches, but what he was really doing was just sitting in dim light, staring at something on the coffee table.

When he saw me looking he sat back against the sofa and let out a sigh. "Come here and tell me what you think of this, will you?"

I went and looked at it with him.

I recognized the gift bag; it'd been discarded on the floor. What Dohwan had been looking at was an ordinary coffee mug—well, not *so* ordinary. It looked like a cheap souvenir from Jeju Island; it was cold and heavy in the hand, too bulky for everyday use.

"Did someone at work give this to you?" I asked.

"Something like that," Dohwan said. "Kind of useless, right?"

No, I said, we could use it for any number of things—to hold pens, or house a little cactus. "How about a candy bowl?"

My husband rubbed his eyes.

It was almost midnight, I said. Surely he could think about this in the morning?

He considered this a second too long. I wondered just then *who* exactly had given it to him, and why he hadn't offered the information more readily. But I was tired, too, and followed my husband into the bedroom. We left the mug on the table.

Early the next morning I found Dohwan pacing on the balcony. It was an awful day—gloomy out, dirty air, dirty skies. I was always too busy to really enjoy weekday mornings, and on the weekends I tended to sleep in until ten or eleven. When I opened the balcony windows the air coming in was so foul I was afraid to breathe it in. I shut the windows again and converged with my husband at the dining room table.

He did his little pour-over thing for the coffee, and I waited for him to tell me why he was up so early. Five past six was pretty crazy for a Thursday morning; usually at this time we were both still sound asleep.

"I'm not asking any questions," I announced. "I just want to listen."

"Hm," he said. I let him finish pouring first because he was intense about his coffee. When we both had our half-filled glass cups in front of us, Dohwan explained about the gift bag.

His father had come to see him, Dohwan said. They'd had lunch together the day before. He was just as surprised, he said at my expression, because the old man had appeared in his office without warning.

"I thought you weren't on speaking terms," I said. They'd been estranged too long to describe it so mildly, but I couldn't think of what else to say.

"So did I," Dohwan said. "And I didn't expect him to remember where I worked. But my father asked for me at reception, and they called me down."

"What'd he say?"

"Not much. People were looking at us. Listening. He's very—anyway, I took him to lunch."

I thought about the souvenir mug, the kitschy thing Dohwan had brought home in a plain white gift bag. It made me sad, thinking of his old man bringing something like that for him, a surprising peace offering for more than five years of bad blood. Not *because* it was tacky, but because a person buying tacky things to make amends seemed to suggest something about my father-in-law that I didn't like thinking about.

"How'd he look?"

"Not much older. Good, maybe?"

"I'm glad."

"He has a girlfriend—he says she's younger, but not by much."

I tried to look impressed, for Dohwan's sake.

"I think," he said, nodding at something I hadn't said aloud, "that maybe you ought to be introduced to Father properly. He's curious about you. He was apologetic, mostly on your account. He thinks he's embarrassed me all these years. He assumed correctly that I don't talk about him to you."

I waited for him to explain—but he didn't.

"This weekend, maybe?" Dohwan said, in a tone which made me think he'd already scheduled it with his father.

"Why not? I have nothing else planned," I said.

On Saturday morning, Dohwan and I took a trip to Ikea. We had a nice late breakfast in the cafeteria, surrounded by moms and strollers and young couples. I spent a long time studying their faces. No one looks more hopeful, in my view, than a newlywed at an Ikea.

After breakfast Dohwan and I wandered from showroom to showroom, looking for some things to put in the second bedroom. I had my suspicions about this impromptu trip, which had come about because Dohwan had suggested it. But instead of guiding us over to the beds or the dresser drawers, he tested out a couple of sofas, gaming desks.

We stayed a long time in one corner, looking at shelving. While he was absorbed in a conversation with an employee about custom orders I wandered away and found a wicker chair. I put my feet up and read a book on my phone. Dohwan came and found me twenty minutes later. He sat heavily on a rattan cube by my feet.

"What's the damage?" I asked.

He made a face. "One mil, give or take?"

"Oh, not bad. What's all this for, anyway?"

He said he was thinking of turning the second room into a proper storage room. "The apartment's not so airy, you know, so I think open shelving is the way to go. Mold."

I nodded gravely.

He told me about his plans, but he didn't think Ikea was the way to go. "We can think about this stuff next weekend—maybe we can go to that outlet across the street. If you don't mind?"

"Of course not. But what's the rush?"

"No rush," Dohwan said. "I just want the apartment to be in better shape."

I understood at once, but I also wondered if he was telling me the truth.

That evening, we dressed up to go out to dinner. Dohwan took off his tie, at my insistence; I wore my new earrings and all of my makeup.

We were to meet his father and his father's girlfriend at the restaurant. It was a great place—Dohwan had taken me a couple of times when we'd first started going out. The decor had changed a bit, but the staff was good, as usual. We were shown into a private room with a view of the river, where Dohwan and I sat side by side. The table looked smaller than I'd remembered them being, and it was chilly. I kept my sweater on and was sitting hunched over my glass of wine when they finally walked in. Introductions were made; Dohwan's father didn't speak above a whisper. I thought he was very cute and genteel, though I wasn't sure if his mildness was genuine. I wondered if the mug had been his, or his girlfriend's idea. She, too, was cute, but in a different way; she smelled strongly of a very licorice-forward perfume and her hot pink dress was skin-tight, but somehow wasn't vulgar or revealing in the least for a woman her age. She seemed affected when she talked—she seemed to want to get on my good side, and also to be seen as a worldly woman. She had a lot of advice for me; she wanted Dohwan and me to have *three* children, not one or two. Or none, she said, as that sort of thing was perfectly acceptable nowadays. She had very long fingers and beautifully done nails; I also suspected she had a good dermatologist. There was some money between them, I thought, probably a lot, judging by the woman's smooth face and the old man's suit and shoes. Even if they borrowed or spent beyond their limits, they certainly lived far better than we did.

While Dohwan was in the shower, I washed and dried his father's mug. It clashed with everything in the apartment; we weren't people who bought or kept souvenirs. I certainly didn't need a memento from Jeju, of all places, to remind me of the wider world.

I, too, had remembered to bring gifts for Dohwan's father and his girlfriend—*very* nice things from the department store that had required a substantial withdrawal from my personal funds. Before I'd met them at dinner and had seen for myself what they were I'd been glad to do it; I'd pictured a toothless old man and his fat tasteless girlfriend, grateful and stunned by their chic wallets and designer fragrances. Instead, the woman had accepted both gift bags without much comment; the old man hadn't even seemed curious.

I gave Dohwan the silent treatment until we were both in bed.

"I don't see much of a family resemblance," I said, yawning.

"My mother was taller, paler," Dohwan said. "I guess I inherited my father's personality." He turned away. I turned too so I could pierce the back of his head with my voice.

"I don't think they liked their gifts."

"It might've been too much."

"Oh, so I chose badly. I see. Understood."

Dohwan sighed and lay on his back. He peered over at me. "Old people aren't showy, you know that."

This was an incredible thing to say, considering his father's girlfriend's fashion sense, *high* soprano lecturing voice, everything-but-the-kitchen-sink perfume, and general persona.

"I'll ask him about his wallet," Dohwan said, closing his eyes. "I'm seeing him for lunch tomorrow."

I waited to see if he'd tell me where I should come out to join them, but in a moment, my husband was asleep.

The second bedroom in our apartment gradually became what it is now: a home office. Dohwan put in a good desk and black armchair; then some men came to install shelves along the walls. It was, after Dohwan was done with it, the nicest room in our home. As was his style, however, he hardly used it after he was finished fussing with it. We did store some things on the shelves, but they were of such a beautiful-quality wood, and we had so few things, really, that the room looked more like a showroom at Ikea or West Elm than something we used.

I thought for some weeks that Dohwan might bring up the subject of moving his father in, but by the time the second room was finished I realized I'd been mistaken. The two were not connected; but I did still think one had triggered the other.

I never met Dohwan's father and his girlfriend again. Perhaps two months after our dinner at the swanky restaurant, my husband brought home some fried chicken and Guinness. We sat together on the floor around our coffee table; I liked it better when we were like this with each other, messy and casual, but we didn't do this sort of thing more than once or twice a month.

When Dohwan was on his third can he admitted that he'd seen his father again, and for the last time.

"They're going to live abroad, in Canada—turns out she's a dual citizen," he said. "They'll be back in the spring. They have to travel back and forth once or twice a year, to collect his pension. Not that he needs it. He offered us free use of one of his rental houses down in Jeju, whenever we want it, it's ours."

I studied him for a moment. "What exactly happened between you two?"

Dohwan seemed to find the question interesting. "Not much," he said. "You wouldn't understand. I don't, either, really."

I used four big wet wipes to clean the grease off my hands as I thought about last weekend, when Dohwan had been away all Saturday on a "fishing trip" with an old pal. "They got married, didn't they?"

He nodded, his lips pursed unattractively as he sipped his beer.

"Was it last weekend, by any chance?"

"They're odd people," he said, after a moment. "'Family only,' they said."

I sat back in a show of stunned silence and exaggerated outrage.

"There was no ceremony!" Dohwan said quickly. "We went to lunch, to celebrate. His wife wasn't invited, either. I mean, to the thing with my father and me. I didn't go to any wedding, believe me."

I relaxed. "I see." I thought a moment. "But you said your father was curious about me, yadda yadda. Or did he take one look at me and go—"

"I don't know. We don't talk much when we're together. Couldn't you tell when we went out to dinner?"

While Dohwan was on the toilet, smoking despite almost daily warnings broadcast by the apartment management people not to, I went out to throw the chicken bones into the waste bins downstairs. I knew I'd married into a strange family when only two of Dohwan's relatives were involved in our wedding but I'd assumed the truth was much more tragic. I hadn't realized his people were simply too self-involved or eccentric to support him.

I'd been using the Jeju mug as a paperweight for our utility bills and school zone speeding citations but by the time I got back to the apartment I had a different idea for it entirely. After all, I didn't need the privilege of a "free" rental house in Jeju, or even the appreciation and love of an in-law, which I now knew would never be mine for as long as I was married to Dohwan. If I couldn't have even that, I certainly had no use whatsoever for a kitschy, tacky souvenir mug.

My husband was still in the bathroom, gambling on his phone and smoking as he did his business on the toilet. It smelled and sounded like a casino when I passed by.

The mug was right where I'd left it in our woodsy little unused office, helpfully weighing down papers that needed tossing. I knew Dohwan would never miss it; I didn't know what kind of person his father really was, but I had a better idea of the son. And the son, I knew, would want me to do just this.

Clarissa

That evening Holly's great-nephew was to come over for dinner. Clarissa hadn't known there was anyone close by. Two years in Holly's employ and Clarissa had heard only the vaguest of references to family.

At breakfast Holly said: "You'll like him, Clarissa . . . he's around your age, I think." She looked as though she'd forgotten what else she'd meant to say and couldn't remember just how old Clarissa really was. She wondered if Holly knew, or cared, about the specificities of her life. All that mattered to the old woman, she knew, was that Clarissa was reliable. Clarissa knew Holly would never become overly familiar with anyone, no matter how much she grew to depend on her. But at times she wished she could make the old woman understand, and deeply, just how uncommon a person Clarissa was, and just what it would take to retain someone like her.

Around lunchtime, after the cleaning woman had gone, Clarissa stood alone at the windows, looking out over the park and watching the joggers and strollers below. It was autumn now and the leaves on the thin trees were reddening; the light was stronger in the mornings, and darkened earlier in the evenings. She was in a good mood, but she wondered about the great-nephew. She worried about what he meant to the old woman, and what he wanted.

The cozy breakfast nook was the most beautiful corner in the apartment, and there the old woman and Clarissa almost always took their meals together. Cold foods were served at lunch; that day it was chicken salad on soft bread, with strongly brewed herbal tea. They spoke rarely during meals, but on this occasion the old woman nodded over at Clarissa. The great-nephew was starting graduate studies at the university in the city, she offered. Clarissa nodded attentively. "That's why I invited him to dinner," she said. "He needs . . . brain food, I thought."

"Very kind of you," Clarissa said.

"Are you . . . looking forward to it, Clarissa?" Holly said.

She put down her fork. "I am. It'll be fun, looking for the family resemblance."

Holly explained, briefly, how that wouldn't be possible.

As she had on the few occasions when they hosted (always singular guests, Clarissa had noted long ago, never another couple, or a group), Clarissa helped Holly into her nicer clothes, then pinned a good brooch to the short stiff scarf coiled around the woman's small, white, narrow throat. Clarissa, who knew better than to dress up, wore what she'd worn to dinner three nights ago (freshly laundered and ironed, of course), and tied her long hair back from her face in her usual style. "His name, by the way, is . . . Albert," the old woman said as they left her room together. "But we call him by his middle name, Fred."

"Is that to distinguish him from his father?"

"Oh, it's nothing like that, dear."

The clock struck six, then seven o'clock. The old woman's personal chef, Andrea, waited on stand-by. Clarissa went in and out of the kitchen, to exchange small talk about the food. Nothing needed reheating or warming, except the plates, which Clarissa helped tong in and out of the oven. The food was the usual bland fare typical of dinners with Holly: soft meat, tender vegetables, little flaky things of beet and potato. To be polite, Clarissa shared half a glass of beer with Andrea, who liked to talk. There was yet another new boyfriend, this one about to turn fiancé. It was a discussion Clarissa listened to with some anxiety, since it meant they would need to find a new cook, probably by Christmas if she'd understood Andrea correctly.

Knowing how the old woman would be about yet more staff turnover, Clarissa tasted a bit of the custard for the tart (too eggy, though she said nothing to Andrea, who was insecure about her baking). Back in the living room, Holly didn't appear too perturbed by her greatnephew's tardiness; though she usually read or wrote in her private office most of the day and evening, at ten past seven she was still nodding along at one of Clarissa's audiobooks, which had only recently been added to their routine. Holly had adamantly been against being read to, unless it was something original of Clarissa's, but one day when they had both tired of reading in silence in separate rooms—on that afternoon Holly and Clarissa had, every hour or so, knocked at each other's doors to ask inconsequential questions about snacks, tea, et cetera, seemingly just to have someone to talk to and to look at— Clarissa suggested they both listen to a book together, as a treat; for weeks now they had been working their way through every Ruth Rendell and locked-room anthology they could find on Audible.

Clarissa sat in her usual chair by the bookshelves, half-listening for the door. The collection playing now on her laptop was one of Clarissa's favorites. The first story was overlong, or perhaps that was the fault (or work) of the actress. Clarissa and Holly each had a cup of warm milk with chocolate as the nude body of a housewife was found in the widower's garden; she'd been strangled with pantyhose—not her own. Clarissa wondered if Holly were scandalized, and closed her eyes.

Fred arrived ten minutes later, bringing in on his clothes the aromas of a city street. He also brought wine, with a little orange discount sticker still on the bottle. "Fred" was of average height, with lots of dark hair and a crooked nose. He was familiar and awkwardly affectionate with his great-aunt, who accepted his cheek kiss but smiled at him only mildly; the explanation from the old woman had made it clear that the boy came from the late gentleman's side of the family.

As she introduced them, Holly placed a gentle hand on Clarissa's arm. "And this is she, Clarissa."

"Fred," Clarissa said. "Though you're—Albert, isn't it?"

"Actually," he said, taking a second too long to shake her offered hand, "it's *never* Albert."

"Never?" she said, wondering.

At dinner they sat across from each other; Fred ate nothing but drank all the wine. He hardly looked up at her or Holly, even as he talked. Mostly he seemed to admire his own hands.

Despite his table manners, having three to dinner was nicer than two. Dinner conversation flowed, and Holly looked brighter, more interested in everything. And Fred was funny when he wanted to be.

To her questions about the food her great-nephew answered non-committally; Clarissa hoped Andrea wasn't listening in.

"What is it you really like, then?" Clarissa said.

"Yes," said Holly, smiling indulgingly. "We'll have . . . something special prepared for you . . . next time you come round."

"Don't go to any trouble on my account," said Fred.

"No trouble," said Holly. "Andrea prefers consultation." She pressed a napkin to her lips.

"Just like Clarissa, I bet," said Fred.

"Exactly like Clarissa," said Holly.

"What'll you do when she leaves?" said Fred. He studied Clarissa's forehead, which was the only place the Retin-A didn't work.

The women ignored his question, which he asked again.

Clarissa talked over him, speaking more for Holly's sake than his. She said she liked Holly very much, and was comfortable with their arrangement here. Fred looked up and for the first time that evening, stared directly into Clarissa's eyes.

"I'm here, I suppose, until Holly doesn't need me anymore," she finished.

"That day will never come," said Holly, rapping her knuckles very softly against the table.

Fred shrugged and drained the rest of his wine.

One week later he was invited to dinner again, though Clarissa wondered if he'd invited himself.

That evening he was only half an hour late. As before, he didn't apologize and Holly, once again, didn't refer to his tardiness.

Clarissa still found him unpredictable and weird, and thought his playfulness was affected. He talked too much. His graduate stipend was "outrageous," he reported, and he was having too much fun doing "exactly nothing." There was a "nepo" girl in his cohort he thought he might be interested in; his advisor was "grotesquely brilliant." He laughed at himself and went on about some other people he knew, two middle-aged women in his program he seemed to spend all his time with but was contemptuous of; no one liked them much, he said, shrugging.

That evening Holly was, Clarissa thought, rather brusque with her great-nephew. It was obvious the old woman didn't really want poor Fred there. He noticed it too, but was too practiced, Clarissa guessed, at socializing with uninterested people to be flustered by it.

For dinner they had cold pasta and for dessert, vanilla pudding and candied kumquats. Holly was clearly displeased with everything, but Andrea had already gone home. Clarissa wondered if the chef was distracted by her engagement plans. The woman would be putting in her notice any day now, Clarissa thought.

After dinner, as they had that first time, they went to talk in the living room. Holly sat with her hands in her lap and waited, it seemed to Clarissa, for the visit to end.

Fred wasn't getting the hint.

After Holly declared she was feeling a chill, she announced she was going to bed.

"Well," Fred said, sitting back in his chair at the sound of her bedroom door closing. "I guess now we'll have to entertain ourselves." He chuckled at his own remark.

Clarissa considered—forcibly—seeing Fred off. She watched as he poured himself more wine. He tipped his head rather too far back as he raised it to his lips, revealing too much of his nostrils.

She opened her laptop so she'd have a clear view of the time. If he spoke to her, she decided, she would reply; at the first slightly annoying thing he did, she would yawn and shut her notebook and ask him to leave.

Fred finished his wine in silence, then poured himself another glass. He left the bottle by his feet; this one, too, had come from the same discount beverage place. He acknowledged her with a nod, raising his brows.

"I *hate* wine," he said.

Not worth replying to, Clarissa thought.

He sat back again, crossing his thin legs at the ankles. He wore good socks, she noted, and good shoes, but his laptop bag was falling apart. Another affectation? she wondered.

"Do you like working here?" Fred asked suddenly.

Clarissa said carefully, "I like your great-aunt."

He coughed. "What do you like about her?"

"She's nice to be with. As you can tell."

He frowned as if she'd said something distasteful. "Is this a permanent thing for you? Your position? Whatever that is?"

"I assist—"

"Right. You *assist*."

She said nothing.

"So remind me: how long have you been her, you know, *assistant*?" he asked.

She told him.

"And you're from around here?"

She didn't know what he meant exactly, but decided it didn't matter what he meant; she explained where she'd come from, and why she'd stuck around.

"That's not how I'd put it," he said. "But I can relate." She waited for him to elaborate but instead he drained the rest of his glass and leaned forward.

"Next question: what do you really want to do with your life? No one would do this sort of thing for a living unless she had nowhere else to go."

Clarissa looked at him steadily.

He finished the wine he *hated*. He seemed to be thinking about something else—himself. "It's a question I'd ask myself. But I figure it must already be in motion."

Clarissa snapped her laptop shut. "What is?"

"I don't know. My life. What I'm supposed to want to do with it."

Clarissa stood and said was *that* the time?

"Thanks for the reminder," Fred said. He had plans, some horrible community art thing he'd promised to be at. He smiled at her acne instead of meeting her eye. "I can see why the old lady likes keeping you around."

Clarissa said she would see him to the door.

"Did you know, before last week, I hadn't spoken to my great-aunt in over eleven years? She's practically no one to me, after all. Then the impulse came to me from out of the blue. I called her up, said a few nice, empty things, then she invited me to dinner—just like that. Lonely old bird. You hate to see it. What I mean is," Fred went on as they walked two abreast down the hall, "we don't really go out of the way for other people, any of us. Everyone's got their own thing going on, and the family—hell, what family? Am I drunk? I can't be drunk, can I?" At the expression on her face, he said, "Fair enough."

She stood still, to give him time to compose himself. To his credit, that was exactly what he did. He carefully put on his leather jacket and took a deep breath. "Good night, Clarissa," he said.

They sat down to a third dinner together at Thanksgiving. Fred brought two sugar-free pies, which was just the sort of stupid thing Clarissa expected him to do. He was riding high, he said, because he'd won some departmental prize and had also been approved for a research grant in the spring. Holly celebrated his triumphs warmly over dinner, though she seemed to have heard the news from another, closer source and had prepared a beautiful attaché case as a congratulatory gift. Only Clarissa seemed to remember the strangeness between aunt and nephew from a few weeks ago.

Three nights before Christmas, Holly woke Clarissa, telling her there was an urgent matter that needed discussing. But the old woman hesitated and wouldn't speak, looking imposed upon as if Clarissa had done the knocking and the old woman had had to come out and answer the door.

"Would you like to sit down?"

"Oh, no. Were you . . . Did I?"

"Not at all," Clarissa said, and waited. The only really old-woman thing Holly did was sometimes she needed more time to find her words.

"I do depend on you, Clarissa," Holly said, and put her hand to her mouth. "But I think that . . . for the time being . . ."

She gave the old woman more time.

Finally Holly continued. "I'll be hiring someone more . . . capable. Someone . . . with *experience*. A day attendant, then someone else for the evenings."

Clarissa had been with the old woman two years but saw now their relationship was worth nothing compared to a new idea.

Holly went on. "It'll be better. For you, too. In case . . . anyway, I require . . . more."

"I see."

Holly nodded distractedly. Clarissa wasn't surprised by her termination; she supposed she was far less help to the old woman than even Andrea—besides, she thought, she was more suited to a big family with children and a dedicated nanny and a live-in cook, or say, to some harried professional woman with double booking issues, not this delicate old bird. Why hadn't Clarissa known to make the correct arrangements herself?

Holly brought her hands together. "I thought, by the middle of the first month . . ."

"Oh," Clarissa said carelessly, "but I can leave anytime. Whenever you want me out."

Holly shook her head, her hand on her mouth. "That isn't . . . no, dear."

"I'll leave everything neat and tidy, just as it was when I first came. I promise."

Clarissa wondered if they'd both spoken without thinking, if they should have discussed things in the morning. Holly's eyes were wet, and she looked agitated, unwell. Clarissa escorted her tenderly back to her room.

"*Fred* said . . . Fred wanted . . . He's family, you see."

"Oh, yes, I do see," Clarissa said, humiliated on the old woman's behalf. "I know how much that means to all of you."

The Last Day

On that last beautiful summer day, Choi Jegil was walking away from his overexerted Kia Morning when someone from the security bungalow flagged him down. "You have to park underground," the guard said. "There's been a—" He pointed at an ambulance floating into view from behind Building 105. "Here it comes. Fire response will be next. You have to move your car."

Jegil wasn't parked in the spot designated for emergency vehicles, but he was only two spaces away from it and guessed they needed the guest lot clear. "What happened?" he called out, but the security guard was already jogging away, in the opposite direction of where he thought the man might head.

His ex-girlfriend lived in Building 101, which was why he'd tried to park outside of 104, for it had an unobstructed view of the front entrance of her building. Now he circled the subterranean lot, the engine of his Morning ticking ominously. He debated whether to park in the space next to the gray Hyundai suv, or take the straight and narrow path toward the exit and out of there, forever.

He drove on, heading down to level p3, and parking, finally, in one dimly lit corner.

He figured Areum would probably be home in about twenty minutes, twenty-five if she had to catch the :48 train instead of the :35. She was not a consistent walker nor was Areum ever reliably home at the same time every day (an impulse shopper, she liked to sniff fruit and try on samples and was, the idiot, always persuaded to stock up on something because it was a 1+1 or a 2+1 deal even if she had plenty of it back at home).

This being a Friday evening, she'd either be home as early as possible (to get ready to go out again) or return late if she'd decided to go somewhere after work. He didn't mind waiting, nor was he put out by the uncertainty of his ex's schedule—if he wasn't enjoying himself, why do this at all?

In the car, with the windows down because the AC blew neither warm nor cool air, Jegil surveyed the underground level and its exits. He watched people come down and go into their cars, go out; he watched them come back in them, come out. Mostly these were couples: the men got out of or into the driver's seats while the women fussed, holding bags of groceries, their children's bags, their own. While he was alone in the car he grew uneasy. It was hard to breathe, but harder to keep awake.

He did, eventually, sleep a little—he had not slept at all the night before—and dreamed a strange dream of the girl Areum used to be and who she might be now. At first she was open and a friend to him, but became altered, silent and unyielding in a way that surprised and displeased him; some women are like this, he told himself in the dream, and this one will never give herself to you. He woke himself with a surprising, yet ultimately untrue resolution: *I'll leave her alone now.*

Jegil was immediately remorseful about his anger in the dream, for he'd never been angry with Areum while they'd been together, only upset sometimes. What'd gotten him, in the end, was that she had disliked intensely being told anything more than once, even when she was clearly in the wrong and seemed unlikely to change her ways, which was exactly the sort of temperament that needed to hear reminders to behave herself. In his memories of her she was always walking away from him, saying to him what she'd always said to him, something like: *but you already said so.* Sometimes the things he thought she'd said when they had been together came to him from out of the blue, sometimes in her voice, often in his own. Now as he tried her cell phone for the first time that evening no one answered but again he heard her voice: *but you've already said so. You already said. Don't tell me again.*

Past midnight he keyed in her passcode at the building entrance (she'd changed it, but he guessed it correctly the third time—it was the birthday of her dead tabby, Dusty) and took the back stairwell. Fifteen flights were nothing to him now, and anyway, he wanted the time to think. Once he was past the third landing he took off his motorcycle helmet and thin hoodie, though he kept his mask on. He pulled a black baseball cap out of his back pocket and fixed it at a steep angle, leaving only the lower half of his face exposed, but as this was covered by his mask, he didn't worry. He wouldn't have worried either way—he liked the way he felt in his hat and his mask, his black clothes, in his leanness and his anonymity. He felt purposeful and also he trusted his purposefulness; it felt like something Areum would trust, too, a certainty that would persuade her.

He stopped on the tenth landing, opened the window in the stairwell, and smoked a cigarette. There were no cameras back here, but also, he suspected the cameras weren't working in the building at all and hadn't been for some time, though he couldn't be sure. He disliked taking chances on anything; he moved as though they might be operational, focusing on him, tracking his every move. His fastidiousness and suspiciousness should have secured a lot for him in life but what'd happened was nothing much, really. He was almost forty now and a better life had never interested him, had never presented itself as any kind of possibility. So far, he'd survived. He'd had a few jobs, a few women. He kept to himself and had kept out of trouble, mostly. That was what he knew to do.

When Areum had first asked to see other people, he'd taken it well, she said. She'd kept herself friendly to him for weeks afterward, answering his occasional texts and phone calls. She didn't know about his visits, of course, his surveillance of her at work, her apartment. Maybe she did, after all—for she'd stopped taking his calls as of last Monday. Now she was leaving his text messages unread. He couldn't guess what she thought of his requests to see her somewhere—a public place, he offered, of her choosing—or at least to talk to her on the phone. He thought they'd been perfectly reasonable requests— after all, she was the one to have insisted that they remain friends after their breakup. She'd wanted him to know that she would always, always think well of him. That was why, even after what appeared to him signs that she'd blocked him from her cell phone, he'd had some things delivered to her apartment—a "luxury" watermelon, two dozen tulips—which had been refused and sent back; his account had been refunded earlier that morning for both purchases.

Not knowing what else to do, he'd stationed himself across from her office building until her lunch hour. He'd spotted her in the group immediately—she was in a sheer white blouse and miniskirt, and her long hair had been let loose to curl around her shoulders like black water. She looked happy and vibrant; she'd walked three abreast with two men to a cold noodle place where they stayed for thirty-two minutes; once they were outside the same trio again walked three abreast down the street to a Starbucks, in fact, the one Jegil went to sometimes because it was several stories and had a good view of the H—Building. Areum came out with a large iced Americano and nearly had a tumble when her heel caught between broken slabs of concrete. She was caught by the elbow by one of the group she was with, an old man of fifty or so who was probably Jang Manager, the one Areum used to bitch about. He'd kept that hand on her elbow long after they helped pry her free and he seemed to be lecturing her or maybe lecturing the concrete, the sky, the birds. The last thing Jegil saw was Areum smiling as she ran her white hands through her hair, her face glowing; then she turned and they all went into the office again; he hadn't stayed long after that.

She didn't answer the door when he buzzed her intercom a third time. He expected little civility from Areum and of course no greeting in welcome, no small talk. He thought maybe it might be better not to say too much at first and let Areum take the lead since he had nothing to say to her except hard, accusatory questions, things that had been driving him crazy. He'd been waiting to unleash them on Areum, get her to release him from the hold they had on him. No, he couldn't waste the precious little time he'd have with her on unimportant opening remarks—but then again, he thought, what was he to her now but a nuisance, a bad taste in her mouth? What could he say to get her to sit down and listen to him?

It was late and he wished not to alarm the neighbors. "Let me in," he said, and pressed his palm over the keypad of Areum's front door until the numbers flashed on.

He thought she might be listening for him in the foyer, and spoke to her as if that were true. Unfortunately for Areum, she'd disabled the tones of her keypad so that even a wrong entry sounded no alarm; he had four more tries after that first mistake.

"Let me in so I can talk to you," he said, keeping his voice quiet and steady. "After tonight, I won't be back. I'm going away, Areum. I'm going down to live with my mother for a bit, then an acquaintance of mine is going to set me up in the Philippines. I won't ever see you again. You understand why I keep wanting to talk, don't you? I'll never set foot in this country again. You won't ever—"

When the third set of numbers worked, Jegil jiggled the handle in disbelief thinking Areum had opened it for him. He half-remembered an old joke the fellows used to tell back in his army days, but only the punchline came to him now: *So the guy says, I startled* YOU? *Imagine how I feel!*

"*Come in,*" he imagined Areum saying from behind the door, "*quickly. Before I change my mind.*" But of course when he let himself inside there was no one at all there waiting for him.

Her apartment was almost exactly as it used to look: he took in the same plywood furniture and apricot-papered walls, her screen-printed ocean views in their large ash-wood frames (in the dark, it really could feel like you were sitting in some beach house, right on the sand). But something had changed—he couldn't quite place it.

The front door shut behind him and, after a moment, the motion-activated light in the foyer went out.

"Areum?" he said in the dark.

Two steps forward then one back, he remained in his shoes, still in the foyer; the light came on again.

He took off his shoes, his hat and mask, his thin hoodie. He set his helmet and shoes neatly to one side and hung up his clothes in the hall closet where he used to keep some of his day things when he stayed over. On a chair in the foyer—this was new—sat a small white handbag, a pair of sunglasses. Beside the chair was a single clear umbrella in its holder. Her shoes had either been returned to the closet or she'd stepped out of the apartment.

He stopped and called for her again.

She wasn't in. Out on the veranda some of her things had been hung up to dry, they were still damp to the touch. On some odd instinct, he looked under her bed and found nothing, just dust bunnies and a hair tie. He would not have gone round, checking everywhere, if he hadn't found her cell phone still charging on her computer desk. It was at 58%. Her phone was locked but he scrolled through the notifications—she had six unread messages (he could find none from himself, an oddity only before he realized she'd had him blocked after all) and a missed call from her mother, from only fourteen minutes ago.

Maybe she'd just gone out for cigarettes? But the handbag on the foyer gave him pause—he looked through it and found a fresh pack of her brand, an old Zippo, and her Burberry wallet. She used her KB debit for everyday purchases, he knew, and there it was, sticking partly out of the front slot of her purse, as though she'd pulled it out and had changed her mind—or had returned home with it, then something or someone had drawn her outside again.

Her path through her apartment was odd; he couldn't make sense of it. She was not the sort of person to do anything in a hurry. The rush outside, without phone, purse, or debit card worried him, nagged at him. Again he checked in her bedroom closet and her bathroom, wondering. For some reason the boiler room bothered him, and he left the door to it unopened. He didn't think Areum would be in there—she used it as storage space for her luggage carriers, emergency butane canisters, and junk she hadn't gotten around to disposing of. He already knew what he'd find inside, he told himself, which was nothing. No one.

He went out on her veranda, opened the windows wide, and smoked another cigarette.

By dawn Jegil had given up on any chance of coming off well when eventually Areum returned and found him there, unannounced, unwelcome. He no longer cared. He felt he would only be relieved when he finally saw her, and actually looked forward to an altercation if one should happen. An argument, even an arrest for trespassing, anything was better than this—because what exactly was *this*?

He was anxious; he was troubled by her absence in her own apartment. Where the hell had she gone?

He considered a dozen scenarios, none of which comforted him. The best he could come up with was that she had found someone new in the same apartment complex, or maybe someone who lived nearby.

He was likely only a short cab ride away (or perhaps this man had arranged to pick her up), and she'd stolen over for a tryst. Was that like Kim Areum? He didn't know—he supposed she could be anybody now. A woman, he knew, deformed herself with each man she took on as a lover. Areum had been one kind of person when she'd been with him and now she was another, and he could never hope to get the former one back for himself. He'd known this as soon as they'd broken things off for good. But the possibility of being with her again wasn't why he followed and watched her and wanted to speak to her; he'd simply wanted to confirm for himself certain things about her which he felt needed to be confirmed. He was merely curious about her, he told himself. If she was genuinely happier when she was left alone, he thought he might let her be after all, as he'd resolved to do down in the parking lot. But first he wanted to see her one last time.

While Jegil waited in her apartment, he watched a cable channel on her television which was playing a marathon of a bizarre American crime show. At first glance he assumed what he was watching was a series of interconnected dream sequences, for the softly blurred backgrounds and darkly lit scenes of people in extreme closeup seemed altogether too surreal to be regular, everyday scenes; but as he continued to watch, the dream never ended. Once he'd finished one episode he found he couldn't stop there; he was three episodes in before he realized he was hungry—and smelled like something rotting away.

He took a shower in Areum's bathroom, using up the last of her shampoo. This was a new bottle of something he'd never seen before, something which promised to "clarify" and "replenish" and smelled strongly of rosemary; it made his buttocks and ears tingle. The body wash was the usual brand she used, a blue-green syrup you had to squeeze out of a hard black bottle. There was a man's razor on the soap tray, a clear tube of exfoliating face wash, her feminine cleanser. The things looked like Areum's things but as he touched them, used them—even the feminine stuff—he couldn't be sure they were really hers. Did they belong to her? Another thought came to mind: Had they *ever* belonged to her? An absurd idea, for he'd remembered the body wash—but Jegil looked again at the brand and realized it wasn't the one he'd been thinking of. This was something containing "botanical microbeads," a liquid that promised to act like a gel. When he looked through the little pond he'd made on his palm he found no *beads*, just a ribbon of black bleeding through the green liquid. He didn't know what any of it should mean, if he was just sleep-deprived or becoming forgetful; it all washed away with one turn under the shower head.

Another crazy thought hit him, something that had been bothering him ever since he'd entered the apartment. After he got out of the shower, he looked through the notifications on Areum's phone. It was fully charged now. A phone that was weightier than he thought possible for this model; it was wired to the wall via a braided cord he didn't recognize. On her screen he found more missed messages, another missed call from "Mom."

It was a bad idea, but he went ahead and did it anyway, using up nine out of ten attempts to unlock Areum's phone.

What does it matter if—

It mattered very much to him each and every thing he did here, to Areum's things, in Areum's home, but he grew tired of his own questions.

He stopped himself before he forced a reset. He knew he needed to get out of there but he couldn't possibly leave this thing or Areum's place alone. Of course he needed and wanted to see her again but also it was something more, something that might explain whatever it was he thought he'd felt since the moment he'd driven into her apartment complex.

Jegil tried one more time with Areum's phone, with yet another combination of numbers. He was strangely relieved when a message on the phone informed him that he'd triggered a factory reset; after a moment, the screen went black.

He put on his dirty clothes then passed urine into the toilet bowl, which he left unflushed. He caught a glimpse of the view out of the balcony windows from an angled shaving mirror in the bathroom; he went out and saw that the world had been thrown into sudden darkness. On the news there'd been some mention of a typhoon approaching the southern coast, he remembered from the day before, but he'd paid it little attention for the weather that week had been mild, as mild as August could get. Jegil lit another cigarette, watching the wind bend the dark trees in the courtyard.

He'd left the TV on the cable channel, on which the American crime show was still playing, but the banner of an emergency alert now scrolled halfway across the screen:

WARNING—TYPHOON WARNING—LEVEL 3—WARNING—TYPHOON WARNING—LEVEL 3—KEEP INDOORS AND STAY OFF ROADS—WARNING—TYPHOON WARNING—LEVEL 3

Jegil got his phone out of his pocket and redialed Areum's number. He knew it wouldn't go through as her phone was still on her computer desk, resetting. Occasionally the screen went dead, then after a series of flashing instructions and commands it stayed on, its screen glowing white. That was when the front door opened, and someone finally stepped in.

Invitation

One night, I woke up with a dull ache in my belly, cramps that intensified when I got out of bed. I turned on a lamp and checked my underwear but it was clean.

Decades had passed so it took me a moment, my recognition of what was happening. I'd been working overtime at the restaurant and was so out of it that even after I realized what it was I crawled back into bed, too tired to even look for the aspirin I kept in my dresser drawer. I was asleep again in seconds.

In the morning, the pain was still with me but it was manageable enough that I could shower and dress and sneak out of the apartment while my parents were still asleep. Like my father, I couldn't relax at home. Though he was retired, he was always going out golfing, or else enrolling in free or low-cost classes at the community adult education center. I didn't like leaving my mother at home alone six, sometimes all seven days out of the week, but the alternative was to stay in and argue about all the little things we did that were so antithetical to the other's standards. So, I worked.

I made it to the restaurant but the cramps got worse as I was changing into my uniform. I had a few minutes before I had to clock in, and got some liquid acetaminophen from the convenience store next door. Panpyrin always got me thinking about my cousin Jimin. She was two years older and had come to live with us for a time. Back then I hid nothing from her; we were best friends as children. For her, my mysterious pre-premenstrual (for I hadn't yet gotten my first period) pain had been a solid enough excuse for her to pinch a couple of necessary items from a neighbor's pharmacy. The first couple of times it'd happened, I'd been grateful for what had seemed to me then undeservedly intense interest in my well-being. But then she kept doing it, thieving from convenience stores and the supermarket and our favorite stationery store. For as long as she stayed with us, I wanted for nothing—there was no snack item, sticker sheet, or lip gloss I couldn't have once Jimin got wind of my heart's desire.

All day my cousin kept popping into my thoughts. I had some time later that evening before I had to clock in again to cover someone else's shift, and, on impulse, gave my cousin a call. I hadn't reached out to Jimin in over a year. Last I'd seen her was when she'd gotten married again. Thirty-seven was young to be widowed and on spouse number two, but after what had happened to my parents, and to hers, it seemed to me bad luck ran in the family.

"Baby girl," was how Jimin greeted me when my call connected. "How you been?"

I said I was surviving, and asked after her husband. I recalled only the vaguest details about him. He was a Kim something or other, I was fairly sure, a handsome man without much to say.

She said he was *just fine*, which, for whatever reason, sounded odd to my ears. I wondered if they were on bad terms. I thought about our family's luck again.

Jimin didn't ask why I'd given her a call, which I took as a sign that she was glad to hear from me, and wanted to catch up. I didn't mention my cramps at all. To her questions I said I was still living with my folks down south, and no, I wasn't at the distribution center anymore. I'd meant to sound nonchalant about working at a restaurant now but I guess she picked up on something. Jimin said all of a sudden that matter of fact, she'd been planning on coming down to see us. She wanted to bring some good salt for my parents, and do the rest of our catching up in person. After all, she said, she was closer to my folks than her own. She'd meant to come down sooner, but life—

"Don't worry about it," I said.

In fact, she added, I couldn't have called at a better time; her husband was away on a work trip.

"But you don't have to," I said, offering Jimin a way out in case she felt imposed on. "It's good just to hear your voice."

"Shut up, I want to come see you. I have all this perfectly good salt that'll go to waste." Then Jimin said she had to go, and rather abruptly, she hung up.

As promised, she came down to see us the following Saturday. She looked good; she brought too many gifts and my parents prepared too much food. I recalled she'd been a picky eater as a kid and little had changed. She hardly tasted any of the side dishes and only had one tiny chunk of the braised short ribs my father had spent two days preparing, cooking it in batches so the meat and root vegetables were tender but the pine nuts and some of the jujubes were still intact and fragrant. I ate twice as much as I normally did for my father's sake.

Conversations went nowhere. We talked mostly about Jimin's mother, though I kept having to pull the topic back in that direction because my cousin and parents refused to ask one another follow-up questions.

After lunch, my father apologized without looking any of us in the eye and said he had an appointment. He gave Jimin an exceedingly soft tap on the elbow, then left.

My mother spent the rest of my cousin's visit giving our kitchen a deep clean. She even did the freezers and all twelve cabinets, including the uppermost left one no one liked, using the stepladder to reach. While I watched TV with Jimin in the living room, I happened to glance that way and saw my mother using a feather duster to reach the top of the refrigerator. Her expression was grim—but she refused to meet my eye. I didn't know whether I was supposed to be getting the hint about kicking Jimin out, or if I was supposed to continue to play hostess until my cousin sent herself home.

Around six, she said she was taking me out for a drink, and then she'd have to head back. My mother was markedly chattier while she saw us to the door. I knew she was glad it was over, but so was I. I saw the apartment as my mother saw it, because having Jimin here underscored what we no longer had: a decent place of our own where my parents could age into their twilight years. I suspected my cousin only pretended to have plans so as not to put us out further. Though we all knew we were just bullshitting one another, she looked properly apologetic about her early departure, and my mother made a small fuss about not doing more, though I thought she and my father had done well; we hadn't entertained so much as a Coway lady in years.

I headed out with Jimin to the only decent watering hole we had in town, which was a chain fried chicken place with beer on tap. It was a five-minute drive along a dusty broken-up road bordered on both sides by shuttered Thai and Chinese massage parlors and vacant medical plazas with sun-bleached For Lease signs and broken windows. I walked this same route all the time when I didn't want to take my bike out but sitting in Jimin's BMW, I was freshly self-conscious about where I'd chosen to spend the last few years of what could be considered my extended young adulthood. I lived in a wasteland that women like Jimin were glad to have encountered only briefly, and no more than they had to so they could picture in their minds what they were working so diligently to ward off.

At the restaurant, and this despite being a Saturday evening, there was only one other group dining in. It meant we had our pick of the establishment but also it put me in a deeper funk about the state of our town.

Jimin chose a corner table overlooking the parking lot, where she took the better seat. I sat with my back to the refrigerator where they kept the pickled radish. Whenever a delivery order came in through the POS, the girl working the counter would walk over and open the refrigerator with such violence that the whole unit shuddered and shook and nearly walked off the folded-over slats of cardboard that were seemingly the only things keeping it from toppling over onto the nearest dine-in customer—that being me at present. For the next hour, during which I felt I could be, at any moment, snuffed out because some careless door-slamming part-timer hated her job, my cousin talked at length about her position at the bank, her husband's financial woes, and her recent trips to Okinawa and Bali over the summer. Interestingly, she mentioned she'd gone on both holidays without her husband, though she offered no explanation for this.

"Are you thinking about having kids?" I asked.

"And ruin my life?"

I ordered another pitcher of beer on the tableside tablet system, hoping to say something to the girl about the refrigerator when she eventually brought it by.

"So," Jimin said, "what's up with you?"

"We already got caught up at lunch," I said. "Nothing more to add."

"Is that right?" She looked me over, a toothpick in her mouth.

I pushed the call bell, again, for the counter girl. "How about some more mustard wings?"

"Okay with me, girlie. Get the fire chicken feet too. You can box up what we don't eat, for your folks. I'm buying." Jimin leaned forward. "How you sleeping these days?"

"Why, do I have dark circles under my eyes?"

"That's the least of it." She picked up one of my hands with both of her own. "You know they have creams for this sort of thing."

The redness between my fingers was particularly pronounced that evening, though the scaliness had subsided. I was pretty good about keeping my hands in my pockets around people but I couldn't hide anything from Jimin.

"How'd you explain these to your parents?"

"No one else noticed."

"Bullshit."

"My mom said something once," I said. "But eczema runs in her family."

Eventually the girl came by with beer and fresh glasses. "And another thing," I said as she was about to leave, "would you take care not to rattle the fridge when you come by here?"

Incredibly, she walked away before I'd even finished speaking. In fact, I told Jimin, "I think she pretended not to hear me."

Her eyes were dancing. "You're right. She didn't hear you."

"What is she, deaf?"

"All sorts in this world, kiddo," Jimin said. She dropped her used toothpick into her beer and gazed out at the parking lot. "There are too many fucking people. A good day, for me—no, the *best* kind of day is to be able to go twenty-four hours without seeing or talking to anybody." She grinned at me. "Besides you, of course."

I rolled my eyes.

"Nothing really matters—none of this. Don't you think?"

"Whoa," I said. "You drunk?"

"Never mind." She reached across the table and poked my left wrist with the end of a fresh toothpick. "You can lie to your parents but not to me. What are you really doing for money?"

My symptoms had been milder since Friday but the beer, or the fire sauce, maybe, called them forth again. I grimaced, which made Jimin scrutinize me even more carefully.

"It's nothing," I said. "Just the old cramps." She didn't immediately catch on. So she didn't notice *everything*. I poured myself more beer.

"You on the rag?" Jimin asked.

I shook my head.

She touched my cheeks.

"I'm not feverish," I said.

"No, but you look terrible. You still get PMS?"

I shook my head again. "I finished my period last week. You don't get PMS *after*, do you?"

"Shit, I don't know." Jimin sat back, her eyes not leaving my face. My cramps were killing me but I felt *so good* just then—it is an entirely different kind of, and essential, experience, when you are warmed just by someone's eyes. It was the way I used to feel when, as girls, Jimin would slyly put her hands in my pockets then walk away, whistling— and I'd find in them a new tube of mascara, or a plastic mood ring. I've never liked anyone else looking at me or touching me, not in all the years since.

An alert appeared on Jimin's phone screen; someone was messaging her, someone she'd been waiting to hear from. She stopped looking at me and I doubled over in pain.

Years ago, when we were children and I first described my mysterious cramps to Jimin, she'd scoffed and asked me if I'd been having *sex*.

I shook my head, feeling very cold. Just hearing the word spoken aloud by someone, and not read out of a dirty book, had been deeply troubling to me.

My parents had been bringing in the groceries so Jimin took me into the room we shared and shut the door. We sat facing each other, she at the computer desk, I on my bed.

"But you said you haven't even gotten your first period yet," Jimin said. "You always get cramps with your cycle. Trust me, I know. So what else could it be?"

I said I'd already thought of spoiled food, cancer, a hard kick in the stomach during physical education.

"Someone hurt you?" Jimin asked, her eyes narrowing.

"No, I just couldn't think of anything else."

My cousin stared at me, studying my body. "Point to where it hurts."

I gestured vaguely down at my thighs.

Jimin shook her head and sat up straighter. She put her hands at her chest with her elbows out, as if she were measuring her boobs. "Not here, right?"

"Lower, of course."

She went all the way down the length of her torso until her out-stretched hands were making an upside-down triangle right where it hurt.

"Here?" she said, for confirmation.

I nodded.

"But you know what that means, don't you? That's where your *womb* is." This was another ugly word I disliked hearing out of my cousin's mouth, and felt sickened, as though I'd been forced to look at a gross photo on the internet. I said I thought my mom was calling me, and left the room entirely.

Some days after her visit, my cousin texted, inviting me up to stay with her the following weekend. She said she had a spa pass, and she'd scheduled appointments for me with her OB-GYN and her dermatologist, both for Saturday afternoon. She was insistent, and asked me up again after I declined the first time. This time, she called. I answered while I was on my way to work.

"My husband's coming back next week, so it's gotta be this weekend."

"Oh," I said.

"And the doc— you need to see this guy. He's a wiz. He'll get you cleared right up."

"This is the OB-GYN?"

"No, the derm."

"Oh that. Don't worry about it. It doesn't bother me."

"It bothers *me*. I don't know how you can touch yourself with those hands."

"Sure, this isn't hurting my feelings."

"You know what I mean."

I took the train to my shifts at the restaurant, because it was an hour away. I'd purposely chosen to find work in this part of the province because it was as seedy an area as you could find in this part of the country, and my parents would never accidentally visit such an establishment.

When I reached the station I said I had to go, and that there was no possibility of my getting off work in the foreseeable future. "I'm sorry," I said. I put on an annoyed-but-smiling-through-it tone. "Let's talk soon, though."

It made me wistful, just for a moment, to hear her sigh into her phone.

She called again the next day, launching right into a conversation she must've been rehearsing in her head: "Why'd you call me if you didn't want my help?"

I'd twisted my ankle slipping on a wet spot in the restaurant, so it took me a long time getting from block to block. My cousin's voice, strangely cold and angry, only made it hurt worse.

"Are you still there?"

I coughed to let her know I was listening, but was otherwise unavailable.

"Am I bothering you?"

I said I was walking home from the train station.

"That's not answering my question, is it?"

"I can't walk and talk at the same time," I said. "My cramps are back. And yes, I've been seeing a doctor. He said it's stress related, and to take antacids. It's not a big deal. Nothing matters, remember?"

Again, she didn't immediately get my reference, which confirmed it: we'd drifted apart too long for us to become friends again. I knew I was being childish, but in an odd sort of way, it was only because I was in my thirties now that I could demand exactly what I wanted from a friend or a lover. If I sensed there was nothing for the taking in the relationship, I left it before it grew to be a problem for either one of us.

"So, what are you saying, I'm stressing you out? No, I guess you aren't. Am I?"

"It's not you." I said I'd just gotten off work; I was tired. She didn't get the hint.

"My husband extended his trip. I'm all alone."

Neither of us said anything.

"I don't like sleeping alone in the apartment," she said, after a moment. "I told Jiyul, but he's no help. He likes thinking I've finally got a problem I can't handle."

"That can't be right."

"You'd be surprised. He's—not what I thought he'd be like."

I thought a moment. "He's very handsome. You're lucky."

"Sweet of you to say so," Jimin said.

My ankle was swelling; I sat down on some broken slabs of concrete and took off my shoe. My hands looked worse than my ankle, however. The redness was darker; the skin around my joints was raised and thick. And everything itched, terribly. Dishwashers were always dealing with dry skin and the occasional rash, but this felt different. Jimin was right; I didn't know how I could live with myself in this condition.

"What are you up to?" I asked.

"Nothing—couldn't you tell?"

I thought that strange; a woman like Jimin would have hair, nail, skin appointments, brunch and dinner plans, galleries to visit, luxury shops to ransack. She could go anywhere she wanted in the world; she might stay at a temple or a detox retreat. The woman she was in my mind was hemmed in only by personal peeves and whims; she was not like me at all.

She offered to pick me up that afternoon, but I still had to walk home. My ankle forced me to slow down, and it took me half an hour longer than normal. I was so tired after my shower I fell asleep in my wet hair, waiting for Jimin. When she woke me, sitting on my bed, for a moment I was disoriented and thought she was a stranger who'd stolen into my room. "You're a mess," Jimin said, turning my red hands over. "Scoot over."

She got into bed with me and let out a big sigh.

"What are we going to do with you?"

"I don't know, but don't wake me up just yet."

"You're already awake, dumbo."

I hid my face in the crook of my arm. "Remember when we were kids and you'd steal Panpyrin for me?"

Jimin said nothing.

"Well, that's why I called you. No other reason—I remembered, and thought of you."

"You're very sweet."

"I'm not, though."

"What would you like to be?"

"I don't know. But men don't like 'very sweet women.' That's what I think."

I felt Jimin moving beside me. She wasn't wearing socks; her feet were very cold and dry. "Fuck 'em."

"I'm never going to find anyone."

"If it's all that important to you, I'll set you up with someone. You should've told me sooner. I didn't know you were looking."

"I'm not. I don't want any blind dates."

Jimin sat up, scratching her back. She was in a blouse and slacks, clothes unfit to relax in.

"I suppose I can get up now," I said.

"Your problem is, you're waiting to be told what people think of you."

"What's that supposed to mean?"

"You haven't changed a bit. It still comes through, sometimes. I can see it."

"What? What are you talking about?"

I lowered my voice; I could hear my parents in the living room; it really *was* like old times.

"I said hello to them already," Jimin said. "I got you guys some pomegranates."

"My mother doesn't eat imported fruit."

"Picky."

"No, that's all you."

"Give me some of your pajamas, will you? It's too late to drive back up now. We'll go first thing in the morning. I'll just reschedule your first appointment for, say, an hour later? Don't you think that'll work?"

I said I had no idea what she was talking about.

"Never mind. You'll find out tomorrow, anyway."

I turned away to face the wall while Jimin dressed. She was so thin she hardly jostled the latex mattress as she got in again. All the time we'd been roommates, we'd never shared a bed. It felt awkward doing it as adult women; it felt a hair too intimate, inappropriate in some way I'd never had to consider before. I wondered if she really was just lonely and needed someone to chatter at in the night. Maybe her other girlfriends were all busy, and I'd been a last resort. I didn't mind that, so much.

It was, maybe, half an hour later when Jimin began softly snoring. We'd been talking about her husband, a topic that seemed to put her right to sleep. When I was sure she was out, I lay on my side and watched her. It was odd—it was, and wasn't like old times at all. Jimin looked too adult now, too made up and immaculate, even with her face washed. She looked, felt, and smelled like someone who could almost be a total stranger.

"I know what you're doing," Jimin said, opening her eyes.

I was unbothered, and kept right on staring.

"You used to do it all the time, back when I lived here."

"I was a little creep, wasn't I?"

"Not really." She turned on her side so we were face to face. Her eyes went from the top of my head down to where our blanket was hiding our bodies from each other. "How are your cramps?"

"Comes and goes."

"You need to take care of yourself. Get out more, see people. Join a hiking club or something."

I lay on my back and reached behind me for the lamp. When my eyes had settled, I turned back to face Jimin.

"I can set you up with some interviews—maybe that's the first step. Then we'll have you situated in the city, put you in an office somewhere, behind a computer where you belong. The man, the marriage will follow. Easiest way to meet someone is on the job."

I thought about my boss at the restaurant, and realized she was right. "I don't know," I said. "I like my work. I like it here."

"It's not about what you *like*, not at your age. It's about what you need before you get too old and people stop taking an interest in you. Turn around."

Just like old times, Jimin's arms came around from behind me. "How's this?" she said. "I have 'magic' hands, remember?"

I felt nothing—worse than nothing. "It tickles," I said, feeling very cold. "I think we've gotten too old for this."

Jimin yawned. "Suit yourself. I'm about to knock out."

I couldn't stop fidgeting; I felt I needed to pee, or run, or scratch myself. I climbed over her to get a drink of water. I spent a lot of time in the living room, walking back and forth, back and forth until I'd worked up a sweat. When I returned to the room, Jimin was snoring softly again. I carefully retrieved my pillow, then went out to sleep on the couch.

We made a late start because my father insisted on cooking breakfast and wouldn't let Jimin leave the apartment without being treated to a thoughtfully prepared sit-down meal. I suspected my cousin ate light in the mornings, if at all, or if she did she was probably the croissant-and-black-coffee type, maybe even a stereotypical cigarette-and-black-coffee style of woman. But when the rice and stew and rolled omelet were ready she sat down and ate, eating far more than she had on her visit a few weeks ago. She complimented my father's cooking, and explained in further detail to my mother about the box of pomegranates and pricey vodka she'd brought—they were supposed to be steeped together, and would be ready in about a week. "But the longer the better," Jimin added, and my mother said a great many things I'd never heard her say before to anyone. In all the time we'd been living together again I hadn't eaten breakfast with my folks in years. I found them pleasant, cheerful, even fun to be around. I wondered what else I'd misunderstood about them.

After breakfast, I slipped off to the bathroom to text my manager at the restaurant about my next four shifts. He called me right away, speaking in a tone he reserved only for young and stupid women like me. Strangely, he didn't ask why I wanted to leave when I told him I wouldn't be showing up anymore. There was some back and forth about how much of my wages he'd withhold for letting him down like this, and he pressed upon me again and again how shocked and troubled he was by my "sudden departure." He played it up too much, even if he did want to make me feel guilty about short-staffing him, which made me think my suspicions of him had been right, after all.

"I'm starting a new job," I said, "in an office. I start on Monday, so you understand why I'd need the day off today, heading into the weekend. I need to give myself time to prepare."

I stopped listening to him, then, and interrupted when I heard Jimin call for me.

"If you won't pay me," I said, "I suppose I can ask someone to help me collect it."

"But why wouldn't I *pay* you?" I could come by anytime next week, he said—if I could spare the time.

"I think I can," I said. "My new employer is very understanding."

The drive up to Seoul wasn't too bad. Jimin was a good driver, and sitting in her BMW was very nice, a novel experience on the expressway.

But I couldn't enjoy myself. I didn't know why I'd quit the restaurant without more consideration. I couldn't rely on Jimin for everything. I didn't know what she meant about setting me up somewhere; she'd never mentioned anything like that to me before. If she'd really wanted to help, she would've offered six years ago after I'd moved back in with my parents. But back then we'd been almost totally estranged. In those days, she wouldn't have even known whether I was alive or dead.

I was so deep in thought I dug my nails in too deep into my palms; I noticed the blood just as Jimin was turning into a rest stop. "Bathroom break," I said, and ran for the toilets as soon as we were parked. Jimin called after me, asking something about coffee or tea, but I pretended not to hear her.

The rest stop was one of the country's busiest; the ladies' room was like something out of one of my anxiety nightmares: row after row of toilets, nearly every stall occupied. I gave up on finding some toilet paper and instead went to the sink to scrub my hands. I spent a long time under the dryer, hoping the red LED light was helping what looked to me like full-blown housewives' eczema. It was between my fingers and on my palms, stopping nearly in a straight line where my wrist began. I'd been staring at myself so long I hadn't realized Jimin had come up behind me.

"Jesus Christ," she said, nearing dropping the two coffees she'd bought somewhere. "We'll have to hit the derm first—let me make a call."

"I don't—" I started to say, but she was already walking away.

Back in the car I kept my hands in my lap. My cramps had returned. I wished I'd made time to use the toilet, but I'd been wary of wetting my hands again. By the time we were approaching Seongnam, I was in bad shape, even by my standards. I curled up against the door, watching the skies.

"You want some air? It's a 'moderate' air quality day, but—"

"Don't worry about it," I said, and shut my eyes.

"I do worry, that's the problem."

Jimin's hand squeezed mine, then traveled up to brush my cheek.

"What are we going to do with you?" she said. This time when her hand moved again, sweeping down across the length of my body, I kept it there.

Little Boy Blue

The boy's mother heard mysterious noises just beyond the bedroom door: furniture being—very slowly, incrementally—moved around, a small little voice whispering to itself, bare footsteps across wood, the clatter of objects.

Haneul lay in bed with her hand on her warm head, just listening. Her boy was up early—or hadn't slept long. It was practically the middle of the night.

She went out and found Yijun sitting in the dark on the living room floor, playing with his dinosaurs. They were deep in conversation and Yijun didn't notice his mother until she turned on the light.

"Ouch!" he said. "Our eyes." He clapped one little hand over his face, then the other over Grandmother Triceratops.

The light was dimmed. "Look here, mister—" Haneul looked at the clock. "*Three forty* in the morning!" She surveyed the living room. By the amount of mess and the height of the elaborate pillow structures around the boy she figured he'd been up for hours. "Couldn't sleep—and you didn't wake Mommy?"

Yijun whispered something into his dinosaurs' ears.

Haneul dug her nails into her left temple—she was either coming down with something, or it was just another migraine—and gestured him over. "Come on, we'll clean this up in the morning. Back to bed."

"Can't, Mommy," Yijun said. "We're waiting for it to happen."

"Waiting for what?" Mommy was amused but too sleepy to be curious. "Come on. You can *wait* in the morning."

The boy stared up at her, his prehistoric people gathered in his arms. "Yes, that's true," he said. "Besides, we'll all have to wait a little longer."

"'*Besides*, we'll *all* have to wait a little longer,'" Haneul repeated to her husband. "I asked him again in the morning if he meant *you*, as in, he's been waiting for you to come home, but Yijun doesn't ask for you anymore."

"I'm getting all choked up here," Taewoo said.

"Oh, you know we miss you," Haneul said. "Maybe he just meant—"

"He's a kid. Kids say all sorts of weird things. He was probably acting out something he heard somewhere."

"But the way he said it—" Finally she succeeded in hailing a taxi. Haneul stepped off the curb and got into the back of the cab. "I'll have to call you back later."

"Look, do you want me to come home?"

"What? No," she said, then shook her head at the driver. "Yes, that's right. I don't mind the surcharge."

"What if," Taewoo said, "I were to head back early? I can probably leave tonight. There's a flight out of here practically every hour."

The taxi driver was telling her something about the traffic on the bridge ahead.

"That's fine. Listen," Haneul said to her husband, "I really do have to call you back." She hung up without waiting for his reply. She hoped Taewoo got the hint. Coming home now meant he'd be returning a week early; she didn't like what it might look like to his bosses, the most junior member on staff taking off whenever he wanted. She left him a lengthy and persuasive (she thought) text about holding down the fort while keeping an eye on the afternoon traffic. They were hardly moving—but with Yijun's school on the hill across the bridge, Haneul could do nothing but wait.

When she finally arrived at H—Foreign School, she was more than thirty minutes late for student pick up. No big deal, she thought; she'd been late before. There was always something going in the afternoon hours, and students with late parents could wait practically anywhere on campus. But after a quick look around the usual places, Haneul began to grow nervous. The yard teachers had not seen him; he had not checked in with his class at pick up; no one had checked him *out*, either. The ladies in administration said they'd connect her to Yijun's teacher but found the number busy; then *they* were busy with a delivery that suddenly came rolling in, a large, noisy shipment of what appeared to be a million cases of paper, with four separate deliverymen who all wanted signatures ("Sometimes a pallet of the wrong type of paper comes in, and they don't accept returns," one of the admin people said when Haneul tried to interrupt their frantic cutting open of boxes). Finally, she could stand the chaos no longer and went out of the administrative building, heading for the Kindy and Pre-K cottages. She could find her way to Yijun's classroom blindfolded ... though of course there *would* be a science experiment being conducted by the AP Biology kids from secondary, underway on the grassy field precisely while she was making her way across it; then when she had safely found her way away from them all she found she *couldn't* actually find Yijun's cottage straight away, for the cozy structures all looked the same in the bright afternoon sunlight. Each had a little pointy red or green roof, and the windows were opaque and covered either in film or with paper flowers or felt animals; at one cottage, the glass was crawling with eerie hand-painted masks of uncanny human faces, tapered white ovals with little red mouths and too-large holes for the eyes. Haneul found herself avoiding looking at these again and went up to the nearest cottage—but found the door to it locked. The next one, too. And the next, all the way down the line. When she peered into the windows she found the lights of each classroom had been turned off. *Deserted!* she thought, disturbed. An odd thing to be so troubled about, she told herself, when of course it was normal for classrooms at this time of day to be shut up and out of commission.

Finally, though she expected another locked door, she looked carefully through the windows of the cottage with the frightening masks—and found herself looking in at a familiar woman. She rapped on the glass. "Ms. Lee!"

Ms. Lee, who'd been on her phone, came to the door. They exchanged the usual greetings. Haneul noticed immediately how dark the classroom was within; then she was struck by Ms. Lee's wan face, but didn't remark on it. She announced instead, chuckling, that she'd "lost" her child. Did Ms. Lee have any idea . . . ?

"Oh, yes!" Ms. Lee said, perking up a little. "Come with me. I want to—" Then whatever it was she was about to say seemed unwise to Ms. Lee, who began chewing on her lower lip. "Never mind. I'll show you to him. He's resting."

Haneul stopped smiling. "*Resting?*"

"He overexerted himself during Afternoon Sing," said Ms. Lee. "In the afternoons, Mr. Gowdy does the English camp—you know all about that. Apparently Yijun was sent to the nurse's office but no one thought to tell *me*. I only found out a few minutes before you arrived. I called Admin so I could reach his emergency contact—you, or your husband—but I couldn't get through. Then here you were."

"Speak of the devil."

Ms. Lee looked at her uncertainly. "I'll take you to the nurse's."

There was a bluish shaded winding path behind the cottages; Ms. Lee led the way. The school gardens were nearby; the breeze smelled of basil and mint.

"You know how *Admin* is," said Ms. Lee without turning.

"Oh, I know all about *that*." Haneul was pleased by all the little beauties of the campus grounds; she bit back her questions and annoyance. "He was up half the night," she admitted, "playing with his dinosaurs. No wonder." She shook her head at Ms. Lee. "It's all my fault."

Ms. Lee glanced back at her. "It's just through here."

They stopped at a blue bungalow. It had a tall black roof and (painted) stone walls and the same decorated windows like at the cottages except here there were no sunny (or frightening) cut-outs pasted on the glass, only black film like the kind they used to obscure the interior of a porno shop. Haneul disliked the look of that film and the bungalow intensely but, as with the masks, saw no reason to be made so uneasy by its facade. She remembered something Taewoo had once told her when they'd been dating, while they were in the middle of a dust-up: *"I have no idea how to understand you. You never make any sense. I know you* feel *some way about something, whatever it is—but that's about as much as I know."*

Well, I don't like it here, Haneul thought, *and that's how I feel about it.* I don't know what it is, or if I can even articulate what I'm so afraid of.

She stepped inside when Ms. Lee opened the door.

At his mother's appearance in the bungalow, the child sat up. He'd been put to sleep on a cot; his hair was damp.

"I'm so sorry I'm late," Haneul said, gathering him into her arms. He was cool to the touch, not warm or clammy as she'd feared. "Did you wait long?"

"Am I going now?" he said sleepily as she kissed his ear.

"Going *home*," Ms. Lee said. "Let's not keep your mother waiting, Yijun."

As she helped him into his shoes, Haneul looked around the bungalow. It was an open, yet narrow space without the appearance of being connected to additional rooms. The ceiling was low for how it'd appeared outside, and yes, even from the inside she very much disliked the look of those blacked-out windows. They were wide and tall and because it was so very bright and lovely beyond the film, it gave them the illusion of appearing like the dilated pupils of something large, *large* . . . Yes, if you really thought about it the bungalow *did* look like an immense head, though of course it had too many eyes for a single face. It was kept dark indoors, she reasoned, for the children's sake. For who was sent to the nurse's office? Children with headaches and stomach viruses, children with cuts and scrapes. Children who needed to be calmed and cared for in a quiet and peaceful place. But there was no nurse inside; she spotted no nurse's desk or nurse apparatus. There was, however, a second cot, and signs of another child having been put to sleep in it, who was then roused and taken away rather suddenly, Haneul guessed; she spotted a girl's hair tie on the pillow case. While Ms. Lee helped Yijun into his jacket Haneul went over to it and picked it up. Clinging to the hair tie were three or four thick strands of a girl's hair, not loose, but bunched together, as if the tie had been pulled loose, and not very gently. She asked Ms. Lee about the second cot and received a distracted shake of the head in reply. "Another child in need of *rest*, I suppose," said Haneul.

That night, she slept badly and woke up while it was still dark. She heard no noises from out in the living room but she sensed someone was moving across the floor. She went out to the kitchen, where she was proven wrong: the living room was empty, and dark. No one was there, and nothing was happening. She had a drink of water from one of Yijun's hand-painted ceramic cups and listened.

Was that a voice coming from inside the boy's room? She thought it might be. She listened some more but could hear nothing in the apartment, only the hum and random soft clicks of various electronic appliances, and, very, very faintly, the sound of running water from another unit.

She went as far as Yijun's bedroom door, where she held her breath and stood as quietly as she could, just listening. One peek, she told herself. The door hinges didn't squeak, and the boy wasn't such a terribly light sleeper. Earlier that night he had been washed, fed, and put to bed an hour before she usually did to make up for the night before. Still, Haneul worried about waking him. If he got up now it might be difficult to put him back to sleep. No, best to leave him be, she thought, and turned away from his door.

He'd been strange and restless all evening (cranky, from his interrupted sleep schedule, she thought). Usually he went to sleep with one or two of his dinosaurs but that night he'd carefully washed and polished then put them away on his shelf. Looking dreamily at her while she read to him, he fell asleep only after she promised never to give his figurines away. "Never," she'd said solemnly. "They're yours to keep forever—until you have your own little boy. You'll understand what I mean when you're older." He'd frowned at this but said nothing.

Back in her own bed she'd been unable to fall asleep. She tried to make herself feel better about the school and that no-good bungalow by making a mental note to ask for a conference (when Taewoo was back) with the head of school and the director of primary. She wanted to suss something out, only she wasn't really sure herself what it was that was bothering her. Ms. Lee, too, though a good teacher, troubled her. Anyway, she'd thought, forcing her eyes shut, HFS was nice enough, but it wasn't the only international school in the city. If they needed to move Yijun before he started first grade, well, that was what they'd do. And if Taewoo asked *why* or tried to interfere, she'd make no mention of creepy bungalows or about her *feelings* at all and simply give him some excuse about another school's better reputation. Facts. Reason. There was no need to convince the boy's father of anything; he'd never believe her anyway.

In the morning Haneul awoke surprised that she'd been able to sleep after all. She turned off her six-thirty alarm and went out into the kitchen, where she'd meant to get a glass of water before checking in on Yijun. Instead, she stopped cold. The door to his bedroom had been left open.

From the kitchen she had a clear view of the child's empty bed. She walked into his room, hoping she'd find him at his desk, playing with his toys: but no child was there to give her a little jolt of pleasant surprise. He'd left some ripples on the sheets in the space uncovered by his tyrannosaurus-print blanket, but the bed was cold when she placed her palm on it. Left abandoned on his rug were his little duck slippers, the left flipped over, beak-side down, the right facing the door. She smoothed over the boy's blanket and straightened his house slippers before heading out of the bedroom. She looked into the bathroom, for she fully expected to find him there, getting up to mischief in the tub or on the toilet. Her certainty about this was such that when he wasn't there after all, sending origami expeditions into the toilet bowl or reaching up on tippy-toes to test the strength of the towel bar, she found herself getting angry. She opened every door in the apartment, tapping on every light switch she passed. The apartment brightened, brightened, brightened.

But the boy was not in her bedroom and he wasn't in the kitchen, the closets, the storage room, or the veranda. He was not hiding behind the washer and dryer tower, the television, or the sofa. He was not lying flat on the floor underneath his bed, or hers. He wasn't hiding in the shower or sitting inside a cabinet, waiting to frighten her to death.

She grabbed her phone and ran out of the apartment, thinking, *Of course, of course, how could I be so stupid?* She ran down the corridor, calling for Yijun. She didn't care if she woke the neighbors; she *wanted* to wake the neighbors. She wanted them to come out of their apartments and help her look. Perhaps he'd even wandered into one of their units? *I will spank you I will shake you I will kill myself if something is wrong, I will die if something has happened to you—*

She called the elevator, then, unable to wait, paced up and down the corridor. She began dialing the police but stopped herself before it could connect. Suddenly she was certain that nothing was wrong: he'd simply wandered out of their apartment. Children did that. Sometimes, they wandered right out of their windows and off their verandas. Yijun was much too intelligent to die in an accident. But he *was* restless. Imaginative and special and charming though yes, at times, too rambunctious, even for his age.

Anything might have happened to him, Haneul thought. Or nothing. He'd gone outside, she reasoned; he'd only wanted to give her a fright. It was going to be a cute story when Yijun grew up, the sort of thing she could tell over and over again without changing any of the details because of how it'd live in her memory. *The time I almost lost you,* was how she was going to remember it; Yijun, on the other hand, would roll his eyes. *The time I wandered off,* he'd correct her. *What was so special about that?*

Haneul told herself she was going find him in no time. There was no other way it could be for them. She felt nothing would ever go so horribly wrong for such a boy; she would have known it long ago. She would have prepared for it. She had never been surprised by anything in her life—she'd said so to Taewoo when they'd first started dating. He hadn't believed her at first, but then, as he grew to know her, he'd understood.

This is not happening. Not happening to me.

And it wasn't; nothing had happened yet.

Go home, you fool, she told herself. The child was waiting for her! He was safely back in his bed. He hadn't gone anywhere. She knew she shouldn't have left the apartment but she hadn't known how, or where, or why to look where she should have looked in the first place. *Hurry,* she thought, jogging back to the apartment. *He is waiting for you to come find him!*

The child's mother laughed out loud in relief. Yijun was there now, waiting to surprise her. Haneul felt it in her bones.

Downpour

In the neighborhood where my friend wanted to meet I moved down hot streets packed with young people and students and couples in light—often matching—outfits. Everyone looked lively and interested in the goings-on of street performers and road vendors. I seemed to be the only person hurrying away from all there was to see. Still, as I walked—and fast, because I was late—I was cheered by the sight of so many beautiful people in their bright linens and sandals; even the businessmen from the office towers put me in a good mood. I liked seeing them milling around in their dress shirts in search of cool drinks, and I liked the looks of the children I saw as they strode alongside their parents in their small white baseball caps and squeaky shoes. Then I saw the man I'd first noticed back at the subway station. He was looking absolutely miserable in his three-piece suit, probably smothering to death in it on what must have been the hottest August afternoon I could remember in years. He was carrying around a brief-case the color of cold plums, which he occasionally raised to his face when he reached up to wipe the sweat off his brow.

Don't stare, I thought. I'd already gotten a good look at his face back at the subway station, but I got a better one now. He had a high forehead and large eyes beneath close-set dark brows. He was, perhaps, around forty. I wanted to approach the man, or at least follow him farther down the street. But I was late, and my friend was calling again. Yes, I was on my way, I said. No, I didn't mind if she ordered for us—in fact, I preferred it. I was nearly there.

And I really was, about four minutes later.

Here now, stepping in, I texted. Where was she sitting?

There, by the plate-glass window, with an unobstructed view of the busy street. She waved me over.

I settled into the seat across from hers, apologizing for my lateness. "I was early when I started out," I said, which Sungkyung laughed at rather too loudly. The metal of my dining chair was wonderfully cold and I ran my hands under the seat.

"I hope you like warm sake," she said.

"Oh, why wouldn't I?"

She raised her brows at me but didn't explain; Sungkyung was always saying things like that, pointing out something she thought she knew about me and feigning surprise when I corrected her. It was as though she suspected me of, or wished to see, some element of unpredictability in my personality that was unknown even to myself. We'd been friends almost fifteen years, and had worked together for at least half that. Sometimes she made me wonder if we even liked each other.

I was still wiping my hands with a moist towelette when she began pouring for me. She looked good; so did I, she said. She was dating someone new; I wasn't. She announced she was no longer going to color her hair, because the shop people were always upselling and she couldn't say no, though she thought shop treatments were bunk; she was considering getting her eyebrows tattooed, again; and I, again, advised her not to.

I forgot about the man on the street; it was easy to. I was in a quiet little Japanese restaurant, where it was cool and serene and smelled deliciously of soy sauce in various stages and methods of dilution and preparation. The stranger passed out of my thoughts—or was sent out by all the normalcy and busyness around me.

I patted my pockets to see if anything might fall out of them while Sungkyung and I exchanged news. But I felt myself growing more uneasy, not less, as I set my purse down at my feet, then, thinking better of it, hung it by its strap over my chair.

"Here, give it to me," said Sungkyung, who would normally have said nothing about my fidgeting. As my purse changed hands across the table, I saw him from the corner of my eye, my stranger.

There was a little concrete island intersecting the main road on which pedestrians could wait for the signal to change, and that was where he was marooned. The resemblance was even more striking from this angle; he looked like he could've walked right out of one of my old family photos.

"That man looks like my father," I announced, surprising myself.

Sungkyung looked immediately distressed, bless her heart. "Who?"

I pointed him out, which was difficult to do as the light had changed and he was surrounded by pedestrians.

"That one?" Sungkyung said, pointing to a shaky old man holding a blue plastic bag.

"No, it's—"

Our appetizers arrived. I gave Sungkyung my oyster, and she passed along her zucchini tempura, a fair trade because I refused to risk raw shellfish. Mid-slurp, she said, "*Him?*" to a pretty boy of about twenty who was passing by our window, a prettier girl at his side. They were both thin as paper.

"Be serious."

"Are *you?*"

I ignored this. "He's right over there, standing there across the street, on the island. The one with the briefcase, the man in the gray suit."

"This is a weird conversation," said Sungkyung.

I looked at the man again and told myself that yes, perhaps there was no resemblance at all: I was just seeing things.

"How you feeling these days?" Sungkyung asked.

"I don't know. Normal?"

"I mean, I know your dad passed, what, twenty years ago? This guy—he looks a little too young, don't you think?"

"Oh God, I didn't mean what you think I mean."

Sungkyung stopped eating so she could stare at me, study my face as if I were one of her patients at her skincare clinic. "Walk me back, because you've lost me." She shook her head in an exaggerated way. "Huh?"

I explained—or tried to. I had photos of my father from around when he was forty, when he died. I was fifteen when it was supposed to have happened. For whatever reason, I don't think of my father as he used to look in photos, from back when he was younger. It's the forty-year-old version I picture, when my father has grown extraordinarily thin, his eyes very large and shadowed beneath his heavy black brows. That was the face I'd seen on the man on the street. It was, I knew, more of a sensation or an intuition than an exact visual likeness, though I knew anyone could see there was a strong resemblance about the chin and temples, a striking similarity between the eyes, brow, and mouth. But I couldn't say all that to Sungkyung. I said I'd perhaps been thinking of my father too much lately; I'd been writing about my childhood, and using photos and old videos to piece a narrative together.

She didn't seem to buy it. She claimed to still be confused.

I looked out the window and saw the man was crossing the intersection now, and heading our way. The resemblance was strong and very clear; this man was perhaps a little taller than my father, but if you watched for it you could see it: he too was not a well man, and it showed in the vacantness of his eyes, the very subtly loose smile about his lips.

Sungkyung called the waiter over and asked if we could have the shade pulled down. I looked out the window at the man as he walked past, and felt strangely embarrassed for him. Outwardly he looked like nobody I should feel sorry for; he even looked well off. Employed, at least. But I pitied him so much and so suddenly my eyes grew wet.

He was no one, I told myself. No one to me. I blinked away my tears and took a sip of my sake. Sungkyung, of course, missed nothing. She stared coldly at me as the waiter fixed the shade all the way down.

"I just don't know about you," she said, which was something she said when she wanted to say something cruel to me and was warming up to it.

"Leave me alone, will you? It's a hot day."

"I hear you."

"You okay?"

"Sure."

"Here comes the owner with the red snapper. He's a friend of mine—didn't I mention it?"

The owner, a lean and very tanned middle-aged man, made his way over. His restaurant was an absurdly tight space, as all these little restaurants this side of the river always are; with the chairs and tables so close together he had to tiptoe around and behind, scooting past diners, rearranging empty chairs out of the way. I thought he might drop our fish but they arrived safely, along with two furry pieces of a "Baja California roll."

"Is something wrong with the oysters?" he said, eyeing my empty dish and the two shells on Sungkyung's. He brought with him the smell of dish soap and rice vinegar on his hands.

"No, your food is acceptable," Sungkyung said, and she and the owner laughed together. While they talked, I took a peek out from behind the shade. The man was long gone.

It rained that night. No matter how old I get, I find myself returning to my childhood self in typhoon season, wishing the rains and winds away. I fear the winds will blow too hard and too fiercely and flatten the world around me, or else whip our entire apartment building up into the air like something out of the *Wizard of Oz*. While it stormed, I stood at my veranda windows. I told myself the worst of it had already passed and was now scattering across the peninsula, as the typhoon had already hit the southern coast. But it seemed easier to believe the worst of it was yet to come. The branches of the new trees planted around the plaza below blew back pitifully and threshed against one another, at the sides of buildings and at cars. Almost no actual people passed by; I saw only the occasional deliveryman speed past on his motorcycle. If I were a child again I could bully one of our old family cats to sleep beside me, the way I used to on nights like these. Instead I got into an empty bed and tried to relax, waking instantly whenever the windows rattled too long and too urgently.

In the morning the city was still windy and rainy but, seeing as the apartment plaza beyond my veranda windows looked none the worse for wear, I began my day. I stayed in and worked on my book, then read that morning's news. Over and over it was the same sort of story, written up by the same sort of woman, a youngish nondescript sort of person (going off her professional headshot) whose contact information underneath her byline was always seemingly some inappropriate or frivolous email address ("snailgirl@central.news," for instance, or "reggaemin@hanmin.net"). And it didn't matter if the write-up was about a married woman in her sixties who'd been hammered to death by her husband (who always claimed to have been blackout drunk during the incident and couldn't remember a thing), or a teenager who'd been harassed or abused or beaten to death by some seemingly mild-mannered relative or teacher. For me the news had stopped being inherently valuable long ago; it was now a daily, sometimes hourly confirmation of my worst fears and my suspicions about the world and other people. And the fact that these kinds of stories were always relayed by the same sort of woman, the sort of woman I could have been years ago if I had chosen differently, if I'd wanted to do better, confirmed certain ideas I had about myself. It always put me in a bad mood, checking the news online.

I was still reading when the noise started up at a little before noon; it wasn't troublesome because it was not an unfamiliar racket, it was only the sound of construction, someone trying to improve their twelve-year-old chicken coop with what sounded like new built-ins, maybe even new doorframes and flooring. The unit on the floor above mine was either letting again or the place had been sold to new people and now—this.

I was untroubled by most kinds of noise and able to ignore the almost ceaseless drilling and hammering by simply putting on my headphones. I worked on some translations and submitted them hours before the deadline; day became evening—somehow I'd worked straight through the afternoon—and realized the noise had stopped some time ago but now very faint shouting had replaced it. This was new, the noises of other people, or what sounded like raised voices. People held a low view of the sort of apartment complex I lived in, but I rarely heard my neighbors and had few problems with the things that were supposed to work in it. I stood in my living room under what sounded to me like where the man and woman might be a few dozen feet above my head; they continued bellowing at each other. Well, *he* bellowed; I heard only snatches of the woman's voice, an occasional *What?* or something else I couldn't make out, screeched at the top of her lungs.

Poor guy, I thought.

It didn't sound like much of a fight. Not a real one, anyway. They'd been working noisily all day long; who knew, maybe they were even having a little fun with each other—perhaps they were testing out new noise-canceling headphones? Or the stress of moving in or moving out, renovating or apartment flipping or whatever it was they were doing had gotten to them. After perhaps a minute more of straining to understand them, I lost interest.

The rains meant it was monsoon season, which meant that on the muggiest days between storms and dry spells, what looked to me like a billion caterpillars made their annual exodus out of the earth or the trees or wherever it was they hid themselves the rest of the year. At the complex where I used to live as a child it had seemed awful to me that such things should even exist; I was afraid of their spikiness, their length and vitality; they were frightfully fleet-footed, and it wasn't just my imagination, I knew, that they appeared intelligently aware of me whenever I happened to be in their vicinity, for they tried their best to swarm me if I dropped my guard. Every summer they blanketed the sidewalks and the apartment playground, wherever it was I needed to traverse in order to go to school or to lessons or back home. It seemed to me then the adults and even the other children I knew weren't nearly as affected by them as I was; I frequently saw them stamping on or even skipping gaily over the black masses of those caterpillars. My father was somewhat sympathetic of my debilitating phobia of crawling things, at least while I was younger, but I knew I might be misremembering, to make him more than what he was. I recalled no one at all carrying me piggyback from place to place; in my mind the child I was is always terrified and alone, her two feet on the ground.

The complex I lived in now wasn't too different in scale and upkeep, relatively speaking, from the one in which I'd grown up, which meant, decades later, that I was still battling my old enemy every season. Unlike the little girl I'd been then I knew how to endure this now; whenever I had to go out on these in-between days, the sweltering, smothering days of the most humid months of the summer season, I simply didn't. The rains would wash away or keep the horrible things out of human view, temporarily, but when it was dry and muggy again they would come out to feed, or mate, whatever it was they needed to do in the open air. Of course, I knew what compelled them, what forced them out. They wanted respite, just as we do, a temporary break from wherever it was they called home. I took walks along the stream for the same reason.

Toward the end of that summer, it was the couple upstairs that drove me out of doors. Over the next few days, the construction work upstairs continued and the arguments did too, though sometimes I heard laughter—always the man's—which was strangely more disconcerting to me than the violence of his shouting. Again, it wasn't the noise that bothered me. And it wasn't even what they were shouting, or that they should do it so thoughtlessly. The answer was much more revealing about myself: it was a little like hearing my own parents go at it, which had, in childhood, always disturbed me because I felt as though I was made to hear things they had no right to make me hear, experiencing hurt and anger and fright though I had done nothing myself to have to endure them.

So I stayed away, and did so as much as I could, mostly frequenting a large three-storied coffee shop across the biking trail whose steep stairwells discouraged families with small children from the upper floors; that meant peace and quiet, and longer hours at whichever table I chose for the day. Sometimes I went to the town library, though the fiction section was about the size and quality you'd expect in a junior high school, and worked on my laptop or read. Their collection of poetry was good enough, and I always found something new I could look through for an afternoon.

One morning I went out without any plan, in my rainboots, armed with mosquito repellent and a big lunch. I wanted a twenty-thousand-step day, which I would normally have avoided while it was so muggy out, but I was growing puffy from all my evening beers and I wanted, like all the little caterpillars out on the sidewalk, a respite, a break in my routine and from everything around me.

That was a day when we were teased by just a little spray of moisture. I couldn't find the sun and the skies were pale but the light hurt my eyes as I walked the few blocks to the pharmacy where I wanted to pick up some ibuprofen.

That was when I felt again for the second time that summer that I had just passed a familiar face. I was waiting for the light to turn when I saw him from across the street. This man, too, looked like my father, though not as exactly and perfectly as the man on the street from earlier that summer. He noticed that I'd noticed him, and, instead of staring back at me openly, suddenly opened the black umbrella which he'd been carrying with the handle hooked to his forearm. We walked forward, two pedestrians between us; as we passed each other, I stole another look.

He had a five o'clock shadow, which was why the resemblance was weaker, and he seemed to favor one hand over the other. As we passed my eye was drawn to his free hand, the one not holding the umbrella, and I suddenly felt very sorry for him. He still had all four fingers; and you had to look very closely to see what had happened to the thumb. The skin on the back of his hand looked thick and mottled but the injury had clearly been from long ago.

I followed him until he stopped in at a Burger King. I sensed he'd noticed me following him, for he hesitated at the door, as if he wanted to give me the chance to walk away and spare myself the embarrassment of pretending I had been on my way here all along. So I did, and walked back down the street. I remembered to stop in at the pharmacy; then I was home.

My air-conditioned apartment was wonderfully healing after such a long time away from it out in the heat and humidity. For once I was glad the people in 2203 had decided on peace and quiet. I went into the shower and cried but only from the eyes, the way you'd cry after being forced to deal with a customer complaint at a job you hated. I didn't feel emotionally provoked, not past the surface, anyway; I was only a little tired.

I didn't understand why my guilt had decided to attack me so late in my life, after all this time, nearly twenty years after my father's death. I didn't miss him so much as I was terribly sorry about how I imagined the last year of his life to have been. I knew he must have sat alone in his apartment, and then when he'd been too ill after his second collapse, he'd sat alone in the hospital. I often wondered what he did with himself while he waited to die, and obsessed over how he might have spent his last days. I wondered if he read newspapers or preferred novels or comic books and if he ever went up to the hospital roof to smoke surreptitiously. I hoped he hadn't thought too much about my mother and me, and hoped also that he'd had friends somewhere, even if there had only been one, the way I had Sungkyung. If in the last days of his life my father was angry and hurt, the way I would have been angry and hurt if the only two people I loved in the world had left me alone as I died, I hoped he forgave me for only now realizing how I'd wronged him. I wouldn't have forced his loneliness on him, had I known; if I could go back and do it over again I would have endured anything, just so he'd have someone in the room with him at his end.

I was waiting for the elevators in the lobby of my building when I saw yet another man who looked like my father, though with him the resemblance was much weaker. This one was far too old, too heavyset. In profile, he looked like no one I knew.

He was on the phone and spoke at a low volume, speaking only sporadically so I couldn't make out what the conversation might be about. For some reason, as I listened, I suspected there was no one on the other line because he paused and started speaking again at odd intervals; it seemed to me no one else was listening to or answering him.

The elevators took too long in coming, and by the time one had been called down, the man on the phone kept glancing over at me as though he knew that I knew that he was speaking to no one.

There was no other way to go about it, so I stepped in first, and the man followed. I stared at his reflection in the mirror, and stared so long and so intensely that I drew his attention. His phone was clearly turned off, or broken, because the screen didn't react when he pulled away; he pretended to hang up and put it into his pocket, then he turned his head to look at me.

"Are you floor nineteen?" he said.

I looked at the buttons and saw that six had been lit up; the elevator was called automatically whenever someone used their keycard to enter the building, and since we two were the only ones on our way up, I realized he was trying to ascertain which ones he could cancel. I told him my floor number, then watched in silence as he canceled the other four.

After a moment, he turned to me again and asked if I knew him from somewhere.

I told Sungkyung about the encounter when she invited me out a few days later. While I was talking she hardly paid attention; she was preoccupied that day and looked round at the other diners in the café, checking out the other women, their handbags, their men.

Finally she looked back at me; she'd been tearing a rat-sized croissant into pieces. They came apart wetly in her hands like clumps of hair. "What'd you tell him?"

I said I told the man I thought I'd recognized him from an old company where I used to work, but I was obviously mistaken. Did he work at . . . ? "And of course he said no, he'd never worked at such and such. I thought he might accuse me of making up the name of the company or something, but he didn't speak to me again. He got off on the twelfth floor. That was the end of that."

"Is that right," Sungkyung said, chewing thoughtfully.

"Let's talk about something nicer."

She said nothing, giving me her *I don't know* look again.

I ordered some more bread and garlic herb butter, which forced Sungkyung to play ball and follow me into another conversation when I changed topics. I told her about a book I was reading on dreams; I said I'd lend it to her when I was finished. "It's supposed to strengthen your belief in your intuitions."

She made a face.

"Trust me."

"Fine," Sungkyung said, belching. "Then I'll tell you about the dream I had last night. You'll like this. Very symbolic. I was lost in this weird-looking city. I remember these really old buildings. They looked wet because it'd just rained. I was supposed to be somewhere but whenever I thought I reached the right address I kept getting turned away at the door."

"That's simple enough," I said. "*'You're not ready to open a new chapter in your life,'* I quoted from memory."

"You're pretty good," she said, looking bored.

She took four individually-wrapped moist towelettes from our table's hidden compartment and tore them open lengthwise all at once. She began wiping her hands finger by finger, stripping each digit of the oily flakes of what'd been her croissant; the rather vulgar gesture reminded me of something I'd seen once when I was a child, some ignorant country aunt who, during a family luncheon or some afternoon activity outside, had sat there holding her squirming boy between her knees, debriding something festering on his scalp. No one else in the family, as I remember it, had lost their appetites at the sight, or even made reference to it. I've always scrupulously washed my hair ever since.

Sungkyung ordered a bottle of white for us and began telling me then of her latest blind date. Mid-story, another entrée arrived. The smell of the garlic and the look of the pale, swollen shrimp on its bed of blackened greens were revolting to me, nauseating. I wet my dry lips with my wine and watched Sungkyung eat; between mouthfuls she described how her date, to whom she'd been connected through an acquaintance, had eventually ghosted her despite their having made out several times, almost having sex in his car in an underground parking garage. They'd stopped only because something petered out between them suddenly, right in the middle of it, she said, like they'd both come to their senses at once. "Weird, don't you think?" she said.

Now that she'd had some time to think about things, Sungkyung continued, the man struck her as a real weirdo. The last thing he told her about himself, she said, was how he had been, until quite recently, living with a girlfriend—now an ex—and one day, they'd been arguing. There was always some argument, this or that disturbance, particularly toward the end, or what turned out to be the end. Maybe, he said, it had to do with not knowing how to express himself. Or maybe his girlfriend had just been an extraordinarily difficult person to understand.

I rolled my eyes.

"Exactly."

The woman had liked growing things—she kept little herbs and potted plants in their apartment. She brewed teas. Something had been coming to a roiling boil, a thick hot sludge; he said he happened to be glancing in her direction as she took it off the stove. They'd been arguing that morning, he said, about nothing important. He'd been sitting at their dining room table with his back to her. At home he frequently went shirtless or else put on a sleeveless tee. All that exposed skin, he said. His ex had always complained about his wifebeaters. How she didn't want to see his armpit hair, his skinny arms. Then without warning—of course there was no warning—she poured the tea down along one arm. One smooth motion; it was over in a second.

"He said at first he wasn't even angry that she did it," Sungkyung said. "He said what shocked him wasn't what she did, but what he kept thinking when he was in the shower, running cold water on himself:

'*It doesn't hurt. I don't feel a thing.*' Later he found out that was because all the nerves die instantly in third-degree burns. He told me the pain comes after, with the grafts and the surgeries, when the doctors try to help you look normal again."

I looked out beyond the café windows, through the dull plastic leaves of the artificial ficus trees on the terrace. I imagined a thin man with kind eyes emerging from out of nowhere in the afternoon light. But no one appeared.

"What happened to the woman?" I asked.

Sungkyung popped a pickle slice into her mouth. "She vanished after she called an ambulance for him. Didn't even take all of her things, he said, just her purse, her identification. He said he only realized later, when she was missing, just how mysterious she was. The things she'd been keeping in the apartment weren't really particular to her at all. Her clothes, her makeup. She'd never been much of a shopper, he said. She didn't even like receiving gifts. He said he never saw her order anything online, no makeup or groceries. She had no hobbies, no personal possessions. When he finally forced himself to deal with what she did leave behind he realized they could have belonged to anyone. She wore clothes in different sizes; he said he wasn't even sure what size her feet really were—he found a range from 220 to 250. I told him that that's very odd. Impossible, even."

I nodded. I was starting to get a headache, probably from the wine. A large party was seated at the very edge of our section; they seemed to be celebrating a birthday or some other occasion. They were boisterous and already very drunk and as I watched, some of the group began arguing about who should be sitting next to whom, whose job it was to gather the napkins and forks, who should get up and grab the vase of paper tulips from the unoccupied table for their use.

Maybe Sungkyung noticed how I'd been picking at my food, or my disinterest in examining her relationship with this lying, burned man and its disintegration, for she got up to use the toilet and when she came back she began gathering up her things, so I did too. I thought she looked odd—annoyed with me, maybe. She paid our check and although we could've walked to the subway station together, she said she had an errand to run and that she'd see me again soon. While we hugged I looked out at the streets, at all those gray city blocks I had to walk alone. I understood just then how Sungkyung could be my closest friend and act as though I puzzled her, as if I couldn't possibly make sense as a whole person whenever she had to fit my declarations and her observations of me together. She could see of me only what she chose or was helpless to see, and any misinterpretation on her part, whether it was intentional or not, was part and parcel of who I was to her. If I kept taking offense whenever I could see her working out my seeming contradictions, I'd lose her friendship, such as it was.

One night I awoke to the thumps and ringing voices of another argument underway upstairs. The woman was nearly inaudible but she suddenly screamed twice—afterward, for some reason, it became a little easier deciphering at least the direction of their conversation, though I still couldn't pick out complete sentences. I could tell from the cold heat in the man's voice and the measured rhythm of his replies to the woman's more erratic, and possibly physical rather than vocal responses that something more would soon happen.

After some silence they started their shouting again; my sleep had been disturbed now and, after a glass of water, I read a book on my phone in bed. I heard the man, who, despite his obvious menace, seemed to me the more sensible of the two, go in and out of the apartment, probably to smoke or just to get away from the woman for a little while. I imagined he was the sort of man to believe in "cooling down" before he did or said something he'd regret, or said that sort of thing to other people as if he believed it. My father had been one of those. He'd tell my mother to leave him alone, to walk away so she'd "calm down"; hours later I'd hear them—mostly him—sounding angrier, somehow, more wounded and bitter while my mother only listened, only sat there looking worn out, sorry, maybe that she hadn't gone out for good. It would've destroyed me, if, as a child my mother had abandoned me, but I think about her now and wonder if it wouldn't have been better for everyone had she done so. I would've gotten over it, eventually. And my father, I like to believe, wouldn't have taken it out on me.

Some days later the noises in 2203 stopped abruptly. I heard no more arguments, none of their usual thumps. Either they'd moved out, or had sold the place and finished their renovations. Sometimes I thought maybe, that night when I'd heard him walk out, the man had done what so many men and women seem unable to unable to do.

Poor guy, I thought, once again.

I was very nearly the age my father had been when he'd suddenly fallen ill, and that helped me sort a few things out in my mind about why I lived the way I lived, and how the rest of my life might play out for me without a few necessary changes. He'd been a chain smoker, but I was, admittedly, an alcoholic. I figured besides our sex and general personalities we were pretty much the same sort of person. I was, like anyone else, afraid of what was going to happen after death, but I was also very pleased with how I'd gotten my life to look, and was unwilling to part from it even in the next ten, or twenty years. I decided I'd have to stop drinking and finally join Sungkyung's hiking club if I wanted to live to be an old woman.

One day, after I'd been running my other errands, I made it to my bank half an hour before it closed. I was the only customer but was made to pluck a ticket out of the machine; after a few tension-filled minutes I was finally seen to by a surly young teller whose thin brown fingers curled over his little keyboard reminded me of all those dark and terrible caterpillars from monsoon season. I tried not to look but soon they were all I could look at, those hands and his fingers; watching them anxiously, I asked to close one of my two accounts and to open a new one that would require monthly deposits, whichever bore the best interest. The teller, who was wearing intensely colored contact lenses, looked mistily at me when I asked about the three-year plan. He suggested instead a short-term agreement—six months, maybe, a year max. He was rather mysterious about it; I couldn't understand the logic behind his sales pitch. The three-year plan offered the better rate, and I knew I could handle the regular payments if I embraced frugality, if I didn't need to take such careful care of my teeth, my skin, and my hair. I said I'd take the three-year plan, please, and the teller smiled at me in a way I disliked, smirking, as if I were going about it all wrong and wasn't I going to pay dearly one day for not listening to him?

I took the bus home, then walked from the stop. It was nearing the end of summer now and walks were no longer things I had to plan my day around, prepare for with sunscreen and extra bottles of water; I could take one anytime I wanted. After the weirdness at the bank, I wanted to think things over. I was in a bad mood, and not only because of the teller. I thought about all the days and nights I would be spending alone at home, with fewer groceries in my refrigerator and no bottles in my pantry. I thought about the money I was hoping to save, and what it was supposed to be for. What I was supposed to want was to have enough in my old age that I could live somewhere on my own, with as many hot meals as I needed and a rainy day fund I could use for an in-home nurse, should I require one. I knew how sensible all that was, but I had no models for it; no one I loved had made it past age fifty. Pensioners and people talking about becoming pensioners annoyed me even as I knew I was being the biggest fool in the world for thinking so little about something which would proba- bly affect me the most—if I lived to join them. That was the trouble, I supposed. I just didn't believe in my old age the way everyone around me seemed to be so certain of reaching theirs.

I bought nothing at the neighborhood shops I passed, though it was the season for pomegranates, for pears. At some point on my way home I saw a middle-aged man on the street and felt it instantly, my recognition of a familiar shape to his head and eyes and profile. I stopped right in the middle of a busy street, certain of a feeling about him I couldn't ignore. Though I was tired and wanted to be home as fast as possible, I stopped in front of a Baskin-Robbins and peered down the block at him. The man stood there lighting a cigarette; he was so thin the bones stuck out along his temples. A black sedan pulled up beside him and he got into the passenger seat. It idled there with him in it, remaining on the curb though a line of cars soon formed behind them, waiting to make a right.

I told myself I was so desperate to find a resemblance that I'd somehow taught myself to do it instantly, to hallucinate the coming together of disparate features in the strangers I thought I was looking at. But I knew that in all this time I'd recognized absolutely nothing: my father's face belonged to no one now, not even to me.

I watched the car until it finally drove away. The streets were dark and I passed no more men, familiar or otherwise.